The Twilight Gate

The Twilight Gate

Rhondi Vilott Salsitz

Illustrations by
Alan M. Clark

Walker and Company
New York

First published in the United States of America in 1993
by Walker Publishing Company, Inc.

Published simultaneously in Canada by Thomas Allen & Son
Canada, Limited, Markham, Ontario

Library of Congress Cataloging-in-Publication Data
Salsitz, Rhondi Vilott.
The twilight gate / Rhondi Vilott Salsitz; illustrations by
Alan M. Clark.
p. cm.
Summary: Tortured by a guilty secret, fifteen-year-old George accidentally opens a gateway to another world, releasing forces for good and evil in the form of a unicorn and a horde of hairy beastlike creatures.
ISBN 0-8027-8213-2
[1. Unicorns—Fiction. 2. Fantasy.] I. Clark, Alan (Alan M.),
ill. II. Title.
PZ7.S1549Tw 1993
[Fic]—dc20 92-22040
CIP
AC

Text design by Brandon Kruse

Printed in the United States of America
2 4 6 8 10 9 7 5 3 1

The Twilight Gate

PROLOGUE

"DO YOU KNOW WHERE WE ARE?" The lieutenant squatted in the dense forest. The air was damp enough to swim in. Stoner looked at his commanding officer and squatted down next to him, his hands still stained with the ink from the map his commander had torn out of them.

"We're over the border." He jabbed a finger.

The paper, sweat-soaked and many-folded, could be read faintly. Vietnam and Laos. Dave rubbed the back of his wrist over his forehead. Nothing could mop up the sweat. His field pack gouged into his back. He felt sick to his stomach.

"We're screwed," his commander finished. He stood up. "They're bringing in fire tonight, and we're walking around lost right under it."

"*Fire?*"

"That's right." The lieutenant squinted wearily. He took off his wire-rim glasses that made him look vaguely like John Lennon and tried to clean them. "They'll be dropping bombs all over us. We'll need a miracle to get out of here alive."

The patrol looked at one another. The war, to them so far, had been painfully shy of miracles. The commander shrugged. "We've got a lot of walking to do."

* * *

Pho rose from his mat and gathered his robes about him. The shadows of the corner had lengthened, cooling him somewhat. He felt curiously light-headed and hearted, as though his prayers had been heard. He knelt before his low table and stared at the sheaf of rice paper, handmade and cut, resting there. His master thought him foolish, Pho knew, and perhaps he was. A young and foolish monk, unlike the sun-leathered man who was master of their Buddhist temple.

Even so, his slender hands hesitated before tying the red ribbon about the prayer papers. He had meditated so long, and fasted, and meditated again, and chanted—surely this paper was blessed and honored. The master had harrumphed over Pho's devotion to the paper, but Pho had done it on his own time. As for the fasting—little enough to eat, with the war going on about them. As for the paper, with ceremony it would be hand cut into even smaller pieces, carefully inscribed with prayers and wishes of the people, and then burned in scented fires, with hope for a better future.

Perhaps the extra devotion he had exerted in making the paper had done no good—but Pho knew that surely it had done no harm. Quickly now, he tied the paper bundle. He then wrapped it in a prayer cloth to protect it against dust and insects. Scurrying footsteps ran through the temple before he'd finished. The quiet scattered like dust motes.

"Pho! Pho!"

"Yes?" Pho looked to the moon-round face of Le Duc, who puffed a little as he crossed the temple flooring. "Soldiers! The long-nosed American soldiers are coming!"

Pho's young heart skipped a beat. "Really? What are they doing here?"

"No one knows. They're just beyond the rice paddies.

The master wants us to be ready in case they bring trouble with them."

Their master was a formidable Buddhist. Pho, packet of paper still in hand, followed after his fellow monk. Before they reached the archway of a door, thunder boomed and the entire temple shook. The stink of fireworks burned his nose. A second thunderclap threw them both to the steps. Le Duc rolled about, tangled in his saffron robes, but Pho leapt agilely to his feet. No smell of rain came to him. This was not a storm that had rolled sullenly over the village while he prayed.

This was the war!

His master kept his monks calmly at the temple steps while screams and panic emptied the village surrounding them. Already, thatched roofs were on fire and buckets of water were being brought up from the river. Black smoke rose, curled like dragons above his home. Pho watched in astonishment. The big, ungainly men he knew to be soldiers galloped across the ground, their guns held in ready across their chests. They were not a pretty people, he reflected. And the noise they brought with them was incredible.

The master looked at Pho. "They seek the Cong," he said.

Pho nodded.

"I will deal with them," the master said further. Putting his hands at ease, he waited for the soldiers to come toward them.

The sky split apart. Red fire and black smoke roared. Pho fell face forward, burying his paper under him. He lay for a moment, ears ringing. Something heavy lay across him.

He felt the sticky wetness drizzle onto him. When he moved, it was with a heave—and the body lying across him rolled limply to the dirt. Pho's eyes filled with tears as well as smoke when he saw his ravaged master, eyes gone sightless in death. Le Duc helped Pho to his feet, the small, round monk crying. Flame poured out of the temple.

Pho snapped to attention. "Water!" he shouted at Le Duc and his fellow monks. "We must save the temple! Master Chau would want us to save the temple!" He shoved his bundle inside his robe.

He grabbed a bucket and ran to the river himself, only half a village's length away. The soldiers met him there.

They stood, in their peculiar spotted clothes, their faces sweaty and dirty, their weapons pointing at him. Pho shook in agitation. The bucket rattled in his hand. His packet of paper lay warmly against his chest. "Fire," he said, and pointed to the temple, to the village.

They seemed to understand. They lowered their weapons carefully and one of them took the bucket from him. He did not understand what they said, but he read the sorrow in their eyes. They formed a line and soon buckets were being passed hand to hand, monk and soldier. The flames died down with sodden hisses.

Two more bombs whistled in, one destroying a small garden patch at the village's far end and the second exploding harmlessly in the forest. One of the soldiers brought out a large metal-and-canvas box with an instrument attached to it and began shouting angrily into the instrument. Then, there were no bombs at all. Pho did not understand what had happened, but he felt the soldiers had saved them all.

He fed them rice balls when they were done. The temple would need a little work and the village more, but it was nothing they could not handle. If this was all the war that came to Pho's home, he would be very grateful.

He wondered how he could thank them for all they had done. As they gathered together and began to follow the river south and east, he thought of all he had he could call his own—and ran after the soldiers. A tall one turned at his shout. It was the one who had first taken the bucket from him. Pho took his package of paper from his robe. He pressed it into the soldier's hands.

"It is blessed paper," he told the man. "For prayers."

The man looked totally baffled and even a little wary. Pho unfolded the cloth to show him, then wrapped the bundle back up. "For your prayers and wishes," he said, and bowed.

The soldier bowed back and took the bundle. Pho hid his smile at the foreigner's clumsiness. He watched them leave the village as dusk gathered. May his prayers and wishes come true, Pho thought. Then, with the prospect of burying his master and of helping to rebuild the temple, he turned to other thoughts.

ONE

"IS SHE GOING TO DIE?"

The question from the backseat of the airport van went unanswered. There was a fraction of a pause.

"I said, is she going to die?" The childish voice went up a tone, now peevish.

The question fell on seemingly deaf ears. Tires churned. A slight patter of summer rain fell on the windshield, and the wipers squeaked back and forth. Someone popped their gum between their teeth.

"Well, I think if she's going to die, she deserves it."

Like whirling dervishes, two bodies in the middle seat twisted around and glared at the small, lone occupant of the backseat.

"Shut up, Mindy!" the tall boy said, pushing his unruly hair from his forehead. His freckles ruined, he thought, a decent-looking face.

"Don't talk like that about Mom," echoed a girl with eyes of stormy gray.

Mindy's lower lip pushed out. She hugged a book and her teddy bear to her chest. "She sent us away," she said from under a dark cloud of brunette bangs.

"She had to. The doctor said . . . well, it's not just the cancer that could kill her. It's us."

"Yeah," George accused. "You've got germs that could make her sick. Then you'd be the one that killed Mom, not the cancer."

Mindy's face paled. "I don't—" her voice choked to a halt.

"Now look what you did!" Leigh glared at George. She reached a hand back to her little sister. "It's all right, Mindy. That's not what he meant—"

"I don't have bugs!"

"Not bugs, germs." George sighed as the two girls clasped hands and held them tightly. He didn't want another scene. Mindy had cried half the flight already and they still had several hours on a bus. "Just listen and try to understand, okay?" Though he wasn't sure if he could explain it, for he wasn't sure himself. "Mom has to have a lot of chemotherapy. What the doctors are doing is trying to kill the cancer—poison it, right?"

Mindy nodded. Her sable hair bobbed on her forehead.

"Now, while all this is happening, the well parts of Mom get poisoned, too. That's the tricky part—killing the cancer without really hurting her. So she gets really weak and tired. She couldn't fight off a cold germ now if she had to—and we're all dangerous to her. A sniffle for you or me could give Mom pneumonia. So she stays in the hospital for the next three or four months—"

"—and we go away," Leigh ended. She tightened her fingers around Mindy's hand. Her sister felt cold. Leigh suddenly felt guilty for having made her sit all alone in the backseat.

The van made another sharp turn. It slid a little on the damp road. The driver ignored them as he had the entire trip. As George sat back, Leigh slipped off the seat belt and squeezed past him. Mindy saw her coming and scooted over gratefully. She gave Leigh one of those smiles—like Mom's—that could practically sprout rainbows. Leigh hugged her tightly.

Muffled, the little one said, "I didn't mean what I said."

"I know you didn't."

"But she sent us away!"

"She had to. There's nobody to take care of us while she's in the hospital." Leigh stared out of the van windows at a bleak countryside.

"Do you think she wants to go see Daddy?"

"No," George snapped. "She doesn't want to die and go see Dad in heaven. Just forget about it, Mindy, okay? Just forget about everything for a while. We're on vacation." He popped his gum again, savagely, and turned his back on his sisters.

He stared at the back of the van driver's neck. The man didn't seem to have heard or cared about a word the children had exchanged. Good. George liked it that way. The Walsh kids didn't need help or sympathy from anybody. He crossed his arms over his chest. He listened as Leigh coaxed Mindy to lay her head down in her lap and rest. No, he didn't want anybody's pity. Just because his father had died didn't mean his mother would. And even if she did, that didn't mean he wanted people hovering around him, feeling sorry for him. He'd find a way to take care of Leigh and Mindy. And the last person he wanted to feel sorry for him was the man they were headed to see now.

Dave Stoner was the man who'd been married to his mother once upon a time, and divorced her, and broke her heart. Not that it mattered to George a lot, because he figured he wouldn't exist if she hadn't then loved and married Christopher Walsh, and had three children. But he did know, when he helped her pack, just like when he'd helped pack things away after Dad died, that this Stoner guy still bothered his mother. For the life of him, no matter how much he thought on it, he couldn't understand why they were going to stay with Stoner this summer until she got out of the hospital.

He had said as much to his mother.

"Grandma can't take you, hon," she'd answered softly as she watched him latch the suitcase. "She's got her hands full with Grampa after his stroke and—"

"I know, I know. It's real expensive for the three of us to fly to California."

"And you're closer this way . . . just in case," Caroline had added even more quietly.

He had looked down, and met her eyes. The difference in height jolted him a little. Just when this year had he grown that tall? Or was it the cancer that shrank her? No . . . both of them had been laughing about this before, the whole last year of ninth grade . . . that he was catching up and passing her. That was before. Now he was going to be a junior. George had fingered the lock on the suitcase. He had felt as if a whole year of his life had disappeared into a time warp. First Dad's death, now this.

Caroline had cleared her throat.

"You'll like Dave Stoner."

George had said nothing to that, but he had wondered how he could like a man his mother had hated enough to divorce.

"It'll be a fantastic vacation . . . and if you have to start school there, it's a good school district, too. But you'll be able to fish and hike and see the country. He even owns a small lake. You and the girls should have a lot of fun. And if you play your cards right, maybe Dave'll let you practice driving. I know your dad didn't get a chance to show you much. I mentioned to Dave that you were due to start drivers' ed."

"So we go have a vacation while you go off to—to get sick."

"I'm not going to get sick, I'm going to get well. This

is the best way for all of us, and as long as the insurance pays for my treatments—"

"Right. Great insurance, considering it was the company that gave you ca—got you sick in the first place."

His mother had shrugged.

He could not tell her the deeper things that bothered him, that she had not trusted him to take care of the girls and keep them at home, keep them together as a family while she got well. Did she know what had really happened the night Dad died? Did she know what he kept knotted up inside of him? And that was why she didn't trust him?

George stirred as he became aware that the windshield wipers weren't helping clear the rainwater off. It wasn't until he blinked that he realized it wasn't rain. He dug at his eyes.

The van made another sharp turn, punctuated by a muffled word from the driver as he impatiently waved to someone to pass them.

There was a thump behind him. Mindy let out a sleepy cry as Leigh said, "That's all right, I'll get it," and George knew Mindy had dropped her unicorn book again.

He clenched his teeth. If she'd dropped it once today, she'd dropped it a dozen times. *Rosebud, the Children's Unicorn*. Fancy gilt lettering, in calligraphy, on the cover. He'd done that. Their mom had told so many unicorn stories to the girls that he had finally put them together in a book for Mindy, for something to do.

George would sooner die than admit he'd lain awake nights listening to the same stories. Sometimes Mom would make them scary and really good—other times, she'd tone them down to Mindy's level, like the time Rosebud had a birthday celebration and a grateful king sent her so much ice cream she'd gotten a stomach ache. He'd listened that night, his arm scratchy-healing in a cast, trying not to think about why he had survived the car accident and his father had not.

He'd done the illustrations, too, on some really good paper he'd found with his mother's old art supplies. She'd given up art when she'd married their dad, for some unexplained reason, and he was allowed from time to time to pirate from the cardboard boxes stacked in the apartment's laundry room. The sketching paper was great, first quality. He'd started doing the book to keep his mind off the crash while he was healing and his father—well, his father hadn't been doing anything, buried six feet under.

He liked art, had always been good at it. He liked computer art, too, and had planned to take extra courses in animation this summer at a local city college. Now he was being sent north and west to some backwoods ex-husband, all his plans disrupted. George leaned his head back onto the hard van seat and stared at the van's ceiling. The storm darkened the countryside into midnight.

Leigh put the book back into Mindy's hands as she heard George sigh. Her younger sister sighed gratefully and clutched it tighter. Then her eyelids fluttered wide.

"We shoulda stayed home with Mom—and made Rosebud come. Rosebud could make her well—that's what unicorns do best!"

George groaned. Leigh flashed an angry look at the back of his neck before turning back to the little girl. "Come on, Mindy. That's just a book, and you know that. Unicorns don't exist."

"They do. And so do . . ." Mindy's eyes, big and round, took on a desperate expression. "So do weevils."

A chill traced cold fingers down the back of Leigh's neck. Not cotton-eating boll weevils—no, this was Mindy's name for something she saw in her nightmares, something that scared her from dark corners and from the unseen depths of her closet sometimes. Leigh always wondered if, in the shorthand language of the very young, Mindy meant werewolves.

The van slewed around again on the rain-slicked road, George clutching the back of his seat to steady himself, as he turned around to look at the girls. "Listen, Mindy. There's no weevils here. Everything's going to be fine! Look, Mom says Mr. Stoner has baby goats and everything."

Nothing would sway Mindy from what she had to say next. "No . . . I left the weevil back home . . . with Mom! You've got to warn her!"

"I'll call her as soon as we get to Mr. Stoner's house—I've got to anyway." George lost his grip as the van whipped around again. "Hey!" This last he aimed at the van driver, the man who'd ignored them ever since he'd picked them up at the airport with instructions to take them to the bus station and put them on a bus that went even farther north than they'd already flown.

To his surprise, the driver responded. "Hold on, kids! Some idiot in a car is trying to run us off the road. He won't pass! Use those seat belts!"

Mindy sat bolt upright in the seat. Leigh grabbed her with one hand and with the other tried to fasten the seat belt. She got it, did her own, and then twisted to look out the windows.

A low, sleek metallic bullet followed them down the narrow country highway. It was a black-and-red beauty, the kind of car that made George's hands itch when he thought about driving soon. It nosed at the van's back wheels from time to time with an angry whine, trying to pass on a road that rain flooding made much too narrow.

"Wow," George breathed. "He really is!"

"He followed us from the airport," the driver said. "You kids in some kind of trouble?" His name, Otis, winked at them from his registration card fastened to the window visor on the passenger side.

"N-no!" answered George unsteadily. At least, not that he knew of.

"It's a weevil," Mindy said. Her voice shook.

"Mindy, *shut up,*" Leigh said desperately. She threw her arms around her sister and tried to brace her toes on the van flooring.

Otis cussed. He wrestled with the van's steering wheel, as it cornered with a sloppy movement that would lead them, George knew for sure, off the road. His stomach clenched in memory of his near-fatal accident and he found his right heel grinding on the van floor, hitting an invisible brake. Somehow, the chauffeur kept the inevitable from happening, even as the car driver behind hit his horn in a loud blare.

George looked to the front again. City lights beckoned. The bus station couldn't be far away. A twenty-minute bus ride had somehow turned into an ordeal. Otis looked in the rearview mirror, his dusky face tight and unhappy. Their eyes met briefly.

"I'll be damned," the driver said, "if he's gonna catch us!"

Once in the city, the rain let up a little, and the day became day again, though it was late afternoon. The street opened up and the angry bullet of a car was free to pass.

But it didn't.

George held his breath. His stomach fluttered. He'd been betrayed by a car before and he clutched the seat belt gripping him.

Otis made a left turn across traffic without signaling. With a screech, the car followed. It gained on them. George squinted to look out the rain-streaked windows and see the driver, but shadows hid him.

The van bucked into an alleyway. The car shot past, missing the turn.

"We lost 'em!" George yelled.

But before the driver could leave the alley, two headlights bored into them from behind. The car had come back!

"That does it," Otis said. "Some redneck bast—"

Leigh clasped her hands tightly over Mindy's ears so that she couldn't hear the rest of what the driver said. Mindy kicked. "Let me go!" Leigh did as the driver's jaw clenched and he hunched over the wheel like an Indy 500 driver.

"What'd he say?"

"That no one was going to catch us!"

George grinned at Leigh's censorship.

Tires squealed and the children went sliding across their seats, to be reined in by their seat belts. They were jolted and whipped across curbs and back streets until, finally, Otis took a deep breath.

"*That* lost 'em!" he said in satisfaction. He retrieved his fallen cap, lost in the fervor of the chase. "And we still got time to make that bus."

George helped Otis unload the suitcases while Leigh and Mindy frantically searched for the fallen Rosebud book inside the van. When the two girls appeared in the doorway, the book had been retrieved yet again, and Mindy's sable hair, with babylike fineness, practically stood on end. Leigh had French braided her own hair that morning, but a few honey-colored ends stood out, and George felt a wrench in his gut. For just a second there, she'd looked just like their mom.

Otis held out his big hand. "Good luck to you kids."

"Thanks." George shook his hand and winced slightly. The black driver had a good grip.

He found his bus tickets and tucked inside were two five-dollar bills for a tip for the driver. He'd planned on keeping them to buy candy bars before they got on the bus, but George figured the man had earned them, after all. Otis took the money with a nod.

His driver's jacket tight across the shoulders, Otis lifted the girls aboard the bus with a single embrace and

Mindy blew him a kiss before running to catch a window seat.

"Hurry up," the bus driver said. "It's time to pull out."

George followed. There was a loud metallic slam as the bus's luggage bay was closed and locked. He found a window seat in front of the girls' seats and settled in. His knees bumped the seat in front of him awkwardly. George sighed. He'd have to get used to his long legs, which seemed to have sprouted overnight.

The bus grated into action and pulled out of the station. Dusk had fallen, and lights came on. Rain sprinkled down lightly. Two hours more, and their journey would be ended.

He'd fallen asleep. Behind him, Leigh's voice reading Rosebud stories had long ago droned to a halt, and he could hear Mindy's gentle snore. George held his eyes wide, stretching them awake, and twisted around in the bus seat to look at his sisters. Gone. Sound asleep. A relief for now. He only hoped Mindy could go back to sleep after they got to Stoner's place.

A white-and-gold beacon lit up the inside of the bus briefly. There were hardly any other passengers besides themselves, and most of them seemed asleep, too. George squinted, waiting for the passing car's headlights to fade.

The beacon glowed. It hung in the darkened interior until his head ached, and he turned to look at the car.

He caught his breath. Not the same one. No. It couldn't be. He looked down from the height of the bus and stared at the car pacing after them into the night.

It *couldn't* be the same car.

It pulled even with the bus.

George couldn't wrench his gaze away. The car accelerated until it was right under his window. He couldn't see the driver, the profile was all in shadows.

He tried not to look. He didn't want the driver to be

able to glance up and see *him*. His hands went clammy. Fine beads of sweat popped out on his forehead, but he couldn't move a muscle. He tried to inch his chin away, to move his eyes. His mind roared in protest at him.

The driver's head slowly began to swivel around toward him. They would soon be face to face.

George strained. He felt the cords of his neck stand out as he fought a terrible gravity in order to move.

It snapped. He gasped and shrank back in his seat, slumping below the level of the window frame, clutching his mouth to keep from being sick. He cowered in the seat, panting.

The beacon passed them by as the car drove on, leaving them behind. George didn't straighten up for a long, long time. Not until he was sure the car was past.

And then he knew he could never tell anybody what he'd seen.

When the driver had turned to face him, shadows had still hidden his face. Hidden everything but the two eyes, like glowing red embers, blazing up at him.

TWO

WHEN HIS HEART STOPPED thumping like a frightened rabbit in his chest, George forced himself to sit up. He took a deep breath and looked out into the rain-darkened night. Nothing.

He'd been dreaming. Or maybe the driver of the car had been from the city, wearing fluorescent red shades or something.

Not blazing, ghoulish eyes staring at him, picking him out of all the bus riders on an unseasonably cold and rainy June night.

George swallowed, his mouth like cotton and his throat tightening spasmodically with the effort. It couldn't have been anything but a dream. He'd just been spooked by Mindy and the earlier incident. It wasn't anything like he thought it was . . . except . . .

Could your own father come back to haunt you? Somebody you had loved and thought loved you?

George wiped his forehead. The Rosebud book hit the bus corridor with a small thump. He leaned sideways and picked it up. Before he knew it, his pencil was in hand and he was sketching in the many blank pages he'd bound into it. Sketching a weevil, that evil man-thing Mindy feared, chasing Rosebud, menacing everything good. His concentration evened his breathing, stopped the pounding of his heart, and, more importantly, let him forget everything else for a while. The half-illumination from the bus dome lights was poor and his eyes hurt. When he finished, he put his head back on the seat and listened to Mindy's sweet purring snore.

Bam! The bus rocked and skewed to a halt with a squeal of complaining brakes. George's quieted heartbeat thundered again.

"Just a blowout, folks. It's going to take me awhile to change it," the bus driver said as he turned on a muted dome light. "Everyone who wants to can get off and stretch their legs."

He didn't wake the girls, but the hair crawled up the back of his neck before George convinced himself to get off. The woods were dark, and the wind rustled through treetops, with just a hint of the rain they'd had earlier. This wasn't any city park. The woods stretched for miles, dark and untrespassed.

But it was the winding road, the road that dipped upward to a small hill and then just kind of disappeared out of sight because he couldn't see any further, that scared him. For as the bus driver cursed and wrestled with a new tire and another passenger helped him, George heard a car's engine.

He stepped away on the road, hearing it scrunch wetly under his sneakers. He heard the roar of an engine, punctuated by the ring of the tire iron and the men working on the flat.

There was no doubt it was a car. Far away it revved until it just crested the hill. Then two white headlights stared down at them for a few seconds, blinding him. George blinked, the lights went out . . . but the car stayed there. It stared down at them until he climbed, shivering, back into the bus and the driver finished the repair job.

He refused to think about it until they reached their remote destination.

Remote was the word for it. Not remote, as in a control for a TV, George thought as he got off the bus; but remote, as in far away from anything. No one else was getting off the bus here.

And nobody was waiting for them. He checked his watch. It wasn't even nine o'clock yet, though it felt much, much later, due to the time zone change and their tiredness. He'd set his watch back to compensate and still was surprised by the hour.

Mindy grabbed her book away from him as she and Leigh piled off the bus behind him. The driver unloaded their cases, closed up the cavernlike stomach of the vehicle, and roared away into the night.

"Well," George said. Mindy shivered by his side. "He should be here soon. Let's go in here."

There was a shop still open next to the bus stop shelter, though the town was quiet and subdued. He was pleasantly surprised to see that it was an art gallery, and the girls wandered in after him. It was sectioned off with panels and temporary walls, exhibits ranging from handmade dolls and quilts to black-and-white Ansel Adams imitators, photos of overripe wheat fields punctuated by rusting wagon wheels. He found himself thinking that he couldn't expect anything more of a backwoods town when he turned around a temporary wall and came up short.

This artistry changed his mind. Watercolors flooded the boundaries of paper and challenged that of the glass and framing. It was as though the artist had grabbed up a bit of his soul and transferred it to the paper. The shapes were abstract, but the emotions . . . he saw joy, smelled fear, fought off evil, and reeled in triumph through splashes of paint. He paused, enchanted. George stared at the pictures, reluctant to leave one to walk to the next. The simple brush strokes, the blurred edges of color washing from one hue to another, yet the sharp distinction of form—his talent was sketching, but this watercolor artist was really good.

A small, still voice asked from behind him, "You like?"

Startled, George whirled about. An Asian man watched from the gallery corner. He was dressed all in somber navy and his coat was in an Asian style, his odd face above the high collar staring back at George.

"These are great!" George blurted, partly from enthusiasm and partly from surprise.

A half bow, of the head only. "The humble artist thanks you," the man said.

"You're the artist?"

Another half bow.

George glanced about the small area of the gallery again. "I really like these." Real, and yet not real. Colorful and yet washed.

The artist said, "The hand and the eye of the painter—that is the gate between the soul and reality."

"The gate?"

"One leads to another, don't you think? Isn't that what you do? It forms in your mind until it explodes from your fingers onto the paper."

"Well, yeah, but—" George paused. How did this quiet, Asian man know about him? "You're good."

"Only if my soul can speak to yours. Do you waterpaint or do you sketch or airbrush?"

"Sketch. Sometimes I use CAD. Airbrushing is neat, but I can't control it that well."

George came to a halt in front of a picture that was almost too dark to bear. It curled in ebony smoke yet there was a smoldering red heart to it that struck clean through George. Tornadolike, the painting dominated the wall it hung on. It had been marked *Not for Sale.* He gulped as he experienced the turmoil.

The artist said, quietly, "Even something as painful as that must sometimes come out. From your soul to reality."

"But how do you deal with, you know . . . having something like that inside of you?"

The artist turned full face to look at his painting. "And what," he said gently, "do you think it is you see?"

The painting had almost revealed him as fully as a complete confession. He backed off a step. "Yeah," George said, "that's the catch, isn't it? What you think you see." He put his hands in his jeans pockets. He wanted desperately to say more, but Leigh's yelling outside caught his attention. "Well, I gotta go."

A third and last bow. "Thank you for coming in."

He bolted out as Mindy began yelling as well.

He saw the man waiting for them. As George straightened, he saw that Stoner was taller than he was. Maybe in a year or two, George might grow that tall . . . then again, he might not. The towering man who surveyed the bus made him feel like a kid again, just when he was beginning to feel close to grown up.

The wind touched him now, slightly, and reminded him of his nightmares.

The man awaiting them stirred. His hair was a thick, wavy thatch of dark brown that went to a silver-gray at the temples. His work outdoors had tanned and lined him deeply, but his square jawline had stayed lean. "It's about time you got here," Dave Stoner said to George, and held out a long-fingered, work-creased hand. He was dressed in rough forester's clothes, no shiny ski jacket here, but a well-worn woolen jacket over faded denims.

George took the handshake reluctantly, thinking that this was the sort of country where he'd have to wear red plaid jackets all the time to avoid getting shot by a deer hunter. "We had a flat." He did not mention that Stoner had not even been there to meet them.

Mindy stumbled behind him. George swung around and gathered her in by the elbows. Her doe eyes were wide and startled and he stifled an insane impulse to yell, "Run, Bambi! *The deer hunters are after us all.*"

Leigh caught the unicorn book as it fluttered to the ground. As she straightened up, George saw a startled look flash across Dave Stoner's face. The man covered it up quickly. Heavy lines furrowed his brow and George wondered if Stoner saw Caroline in her youth, followed by George's own startled thought that his mother couldn't possibly be as old as this guy.

Stoner pulled them all into the lee of the shelter, out of the late spring night's chill. "How is Carrie?" asked his mother's first husband.

George thought that not only would he never be that tall, but he would never have a voice that deep. "Carrie? Ah . . . oh, you mean Mom." George stammered to a halt.

"Her friends call her Caroline," Leigh said. Disapproval stained her words.

Before George could kick her in the ankle for being hostile, Mindy said, "I thought you guys told me we had to like Mr. Stoner."

A wry smile pulled the right corner of the man's mouth. "It's too late to decide things like that," he said. "Let's get your suitcases and go home."

Finally George had something to do that he knew he could handle. He got two out of the three cases and balanced them on either side of his lean body, even though their weight hurt his shoulders. Stoner gave him an amused glance, picked up Mindy's small bag, and led the way to the car.

Not a car, really. George swallowed a relieved sigh that it wasn't the red-and-black bullet that had been haunting him. This was a four-wheeler, with old mud splattered up its sides, and great treaded tires resting solidly on the ground. George piled the suitcases into the back with a grunt, then hauled himself into the front seat, where he'd finally have some leg room.

Leigh hesitated, then let Stoner help her into the backseat. Mindy stood her ground, marshaling her teddy bear and her book, eyeing the tall man. "I suppose," she said, "you can touch me."

Solemnly, the man bent and lifted her into the backseat. He brushed Leigh's hands aside gently and fastened the seat belt himself. He tapped the cover of the book.

"What's that?"

"My brother made it for me," Mindy said. She thrust the

book at him as both George and Leigh sucked in their breath. Their sister didn't let strangers touch the unicorn book.

He opened it. George looked away, unable to bear criticism. His unicorns had always been fantastic creatures, not delicate or whimsical, but massive creatures of righteous anger, fire, and light.

Stoner nodded. "Carrie always liked to draw unicorns, too." He closed the book carefully. "Maybe I can look at it later. We've a long drive back to the cabin."

"Cabin?"

"That's right." He shut the door carefully, blocking out Mindy's delighted expression.

She settled back onto the old Naugahyde seat with a satisfied hop. "A cabin!" she declared, as Stoner climbed in and started the vehicle.

Leigh woke first in the morning, as always. During the night, Mindy had pressed into the small of her back, her skin as warm as a tiny furnace. Leigh shifted in the bed and crawled out carefully and pushed her pillow into the warm dimple of the bed, and Mindy snuggled into it with a tiny sigh.

She pulled on her jeans and a long-sleeved T-shirt quickly. Without being aware of it consciously, she'd remembered long before waking that she was somewhere strange. Now she crept cautiously about the loft bedroom. She looked over the low wall that opened out onto the big downstairs living room. No one was to be seen, but she sniffed. Someone had coffee brewing. Leigh liked the smell of coffee, though when she could sneak a cup, she liked lots of milk and sugar in it.

If she'd been younger, the loft bedroom would have pleased her tremendously, she thought as she stood a moment in the doorframe. The big double bed was a four-poster, and a huge quilt reigned in place of a bedspread. There was a wide window, now shuttered, to the forest beyond. The only thing disagreeable about the loft was the half wall. Well, she'd just have to dress and undress hunched over, or maybe in the bathroom. The lack of privacy was bad, but she'd have to find a way to work with it.

Worse was the rapidly changing status of her own body. The last thing she wanted right now was to be a thousand miles away from her mother . . . just in case she had to ask some questions.

Leigh sighed, ran her hand through her dark honey-colored hair, which was all ripply from having been in a braid all the day before, and shut the bedroom door quietly behind her.

The house wasn't really a cabin . . . well, it was and it wasn't. A huge, rough wood-and-stone house, it had two bedrooms and a loft upstairs, and the whole bottom was a big kitchen and living room. Mr. Stoner had let George have the regular bedroom—the second was a study she'd peeked at, filled with books and piles of papers and a broken-down couch, and that's where he would sleep. That left the loft for the two girls.

At least Mindy hadn't been disappointed when they'd driven up last night. She'd drunk some hot chocolate and fallen asleep even before they'd called to let their mom know they'd made it. Leigh winced at the memory. Mom had sounded really weak and sick to her stomach. She'd had a treatment right after they left for the airport, and chemotherapy always made her really sick. Leigh balled her hand. She shouldn't have left her mother alone.

She paused on the stairs as two deep voices murmuring reached her. So Mr. Stoner was up—and he had company. Leigh hesitated. She hated meeting new people. Even worse was the look in their eyes now as they shook her hand. *Oh, so you're the little girl whose mother has cancer and is dying. What a pity*, they always seemed to say without saying it out loud.

Leigh stepped down onto the stone flooring of the living room. Its chill went right through her socks. She stared down in surprise, then remembered that although summer was but a few days away, this was farther north than she'd ever been, close to the Canadian border.

The great silver-and-black wolflike dog lying near the hearth got up and padded over to her. They'd met last night, but Leigh hesitated as she stretched her hand out.

Wolf sniffed her, his nose and muzzle wet. His slanted eyes warmed and he pressed close to her legs. She buried her fingers in his thick coat and he walked with her to the kitchen.

A man was saying, with a lilting accent that reminded Leigh of the Muppet character the Swedish Chef, ". . . I didn't think it was Wolf, but I wanted to check with you. Never seen anything like it, Dave. Better keep those two kids of yours inside the shed at night or you'll lose them, too."

Two kids, Leigh thought. *Make that three! And we don't want to sleep in any old shed!*

A chair scraped. "The goats are just to help Carrie's family settle in, but I'll keep them penned up. Wouldn't want the little girls to find them slaughtered in the backyard. Think we have some wild dogs on our hands?"

Leigh pressed her fingers to her lips as she grew to understand.

"Maybe. But I just can't figure out how they got through the fencing. An' th' little one was drained of blood."

Leigh was still sorting out what she'd overheard when Wolf pressed her into the kitchen itself, and Dave Stoner saw her in the doorway. His heavy frown lightened.

"Well. Here's an early riser now. Eric, I'd like you to meet Leigh. Leigh, this is Mr. Johannsen, a neighbor of ours."

She blurted out, "Did something get killed at your house?" then bit her lower lip and felt her face flood with warmth.

The big, fair-skinned man occupying one whole side of the kitchen table nodded. "Ja, sure enough. I lost a prize ewe and her weanling. My son was counting on getting that one ready for th' fair." He held out a big, beefy hand. "Pleased to meet you, flicka."

"Flicka . . . like the book. It means girl, right?"

"That's right."

Stoner stood up. "What can I get you, Leigh? Oatmeal? Fry an egg?"

She inhaled deeply. "A cup of coffee?"

They considered one another. Then Stoner said, "Your mom lets you drink coffee?"

"Sometimes."

He nodded. "Fair enough. Sugar's out on the counter. When the others get up, though, I expect you to eat a little something."

"I will."

Johannsen laughed. "Bring her over to my house. Momma wants to meet all of them as soon as possible." The big American Swede didn't seem to notice the challenge Stoner had just given her, and that she'd passed, Leigh thought as she went around the table and found a stoneware mug.

With a pleased snort, Wolf went and lay down in the corner. Upstairs, the floor creaked and Stoner looked up.

"Sounds like George is up, too."

Leigh ducked her head as she realized that the two men must have heard her walking around upstairs as well. She hoped that they didn't think she'd been eavesdropping.

She mixed the coffee to a very light, mellow brown and stirred in two teaspoons of sugar. The mug steamed, and the spoon warmed between her fingers. She sat down at the table and wrapped her hands about the cup. Despite all the milk, she could only sip a little at a time.

George came down the stairs fairly rattling each step. He came into the kitchen, all arms and legs. His face was scraped a bright pink on both sides from shaving before he came down.

Her brother was hard to figure out. Most of the time he teased and mocked her, but Mom had told her it was just his way to break clear of the family—of separating the kids from the grown-ups. She hated it, though, and more often than not, cheerfully hated him. George seemed to hate her for not missing their father more, but Leigh hadn't liked their dad and couldn't miss him. George had changed a lot since the accident. As she looked down into her café au lait, she remembered, with a jolt, that when she had been Mindy's age, she'd followed him all around like a puppy.

George didn't even ask if he could have coffee. He poured a big foaming glass of milk and set about frying himself some eggs. Stoner wore a funny expression as he looked at him over his shoulder, and Johannsen grinned.

Well, that was George for you. *Just walk right in and make yourself at home*, Leigh thought. She took another cautious sip of her drink. Though George had been a little strange last night. Quiet and pale. She wondered if he had been scared about leaving Mom, too.

"George, this is Eric Johannsen."

George waved a haughty hello with the pancake turner. "Good morning." Then he added, as if in explanation, "I'm starved."

Stoner said dryly, "It looks like you're taking care of it."

"Want me to make you some, too? I can do over easy, sunny-side up . . . scrambled, if you've got cheese. Mindy always takes her eggs scrambled."

Stoner took that in. Leigh could almost see him taking mental notes again, the way he'd been doing all last night. Then she realized that he was trying to learn about them—what they liked and didn't, and how their mother expected him to take care of them. Almost as if he really cared, and they weren't just some sort of freaky burden dumped on him.

Johannsen stood up. Half the kitchen seemed to fill with the size of him, as eggs sizzled in the frying pan. "Got to go. Take care of those kids, now, eh? And the children as well." His amused gaze passed over Leigh and she blushed. How had he known?

"Tell Inga I'll bring 'em by tomorrow, but I'll call first."

"Good." He leaned over Leigh. "You like horses, little flicka?"

"Yes." Her heart soared. Did this big man have horses?

His pale blue eyes stared into hers. "Then you'll like our woods. Let me know if you see the ghost mare, too. Stoner here makes fun of me—but I've seen her."

"Ghost mare?"

"It's an Indian legend," Stoner said, a little too loudly. "A white spirit mare, a medicine animal. Come on, Eric. That's only the dairy farm's retired delivery mare you see . . . and you know it as well as I."

Leigh deflated.

The big Swede laughed, but he touched her shoulder gently. "Leigh and I, we know better. Well, now, good-bye to you, tall George, as well." With that, he was gone, and the house seemed very empty for a few seconds as the back door rattled behind him.

Wolf got up, sniffed at the door, and returned to his corner.

A thin shriek wailed through the upstairs.

"Oh, cripes," George said. He shoved the frying pan to a back burner and made it up the stairs just before Leigh and Stoner.

Mindy stood before the open window, dwarfed by one of Leigh's nightgowns because they hadn't been able to find hers last night. She had unlatched and thrown the shutters wide. She pointed down to the woods.

"I saw it! There!"

"That was just a friend of Mr. Stoner's," George said. "What are you scared about?" He took a menacing step toward Mindy, unwilling to deal with her nightmares this morning.

Leigh felt a tug inside and brushed past him. She took her sister in her arms. "What did you see, baby?" she asked, hearing an echo of their mom in her own voice.

"Rosebud! I saw Rosebud in the woods!"

Rosebud

THREE

STONER TOWERED OVER MINDY. The oversized nightgown billowed around her trembling body like a vast, white sail. His lips tightened and he looked out the window.

"What's she screaming about?"

"She thinks she saw Rosebud—the unicorn in her book." Leigh hugged Mindy closer. How could the warm little person she'd left behind in the bed have gotten so icy cold?

"I did see her! And she was big, and white, and she reared when she saw me looking down at her from the window."

Stoner mumbled something. He swung around on one heel and charged into his study, the door banging loudly behind him. George heard the rapid tones of a telephone being dialed and raised an eyebrow at Leigh. She stroked Mindy's hair and tried to soothe her excited sister.

The deep voice vibrated through the wall clearly. "Hey, Micah. This is Dave Stoner. Did that old mare of yours get loose again? I think I saw her grazing down by my house this morning. She loves that old pastureland of mine."

With a faint blush, Leigh made a note to herself about the privacy of her new room as she heard his voice clearly.

"Since yesterday, huh. Well, if I get my hands on her, I'll ring you up. You can pick her up after dinner. Right. Thanks, Micah."

Despite Mindy's sigh of disappointment, Leigh looked out the window. A horse . . . even a placid old mare . . . right in her backyard!

George shuffled his feet impatiently. He had been hoping beyond hope that his sisters would not embarrass him. Now Mindy was starting. "See, Mindy? It's just an old horse."

"Was not."

"Come on, Mindy." George's patience evaporated.

Leigh steered her away. "Get dressed and come down to get breakfast. Maybe we can go out and look for it, if it's lost. Maybe Mr. Stoner will let us—" She broke off as Dave Stoner filled the doorway again.

He scratched his chin. "Look, you can't spend all summer here calling me mister. It's Stoner, okay? Dave, if you're really desperate." He approached Mindy and leaned down. "The old mare's name is Daisy. The sooner you get dressed, the sooner we can find her—and I think she wouldn't mind giving a ride to a little bit like you." He craned his neck to take in Leigh's expression. "Your sister's about the right size for her, too." The older girl went red in the face.

"Don't do me any favors," Leigh muttered to herself as she left Mindy smiling angelically at Stoner, and went to lay out fresh clothes for her sister.

George took a deep breath. Leigh didn't like anyone knowing her secrets, her inner self. He didn't blame her. He hid a shudder as he thought about anyone knowing *his*.

The rangy man knelt near the fallen fence post of the open pasture. "There's no sign." Dave Stoner frowned at the grounds. He looked back up at the stone house, eyeing the loft bedroom window. "Are you sure this is where you saw it?"

Mindy pressed her book to her chest and nodded firmly. Leigh sighed while George ignored all of them in disgust. His fingers twitched and Leigh knew he was sketching in his mind, drawing caricatures of all of them, filled with that ugly impatience her brother had had ever since he turned fourteen. Wolf took the expedition in joyous doglike delirium. The beast romped through the meadow grasses, jumping at the children one by one.

Leigh hugged herself in anticipation, thinking, *A horse!* and looked to the edge of the forest eagerly. Wolf tagged her ankle, gave a foolish bark, and rolled in the grass. She knelt over to rub his silver-and-charcoal stomach.

"Think, Mindy."

"This is where I saw Rosebud." Mindy's chin dimpled in determination.

Stoner kicked the ground. "Well, I suggest we spread out." He inhaled deeply.

He'd beaten George in a footrace out to the meadows. It gave George only a little satisfaction that the man was breathing harder than he was. George scuffled. He watched the brown-edged and graying trees, aware of a problem within these woods. The evergreens and conifers looked under siege, battling to stay alive. "What's beyond here?"

"Spirit Lake, about ten miles down the road."

"That the lake you own?"

"Sort of."

"How can you own a whole lake?" Leigh tilted her head.

"It was Indian land . . . my great-grandfather was what you call a white Indian. He was the only one left. Now I am."

"Can we go?"

"It's not . . . healthy," Stoner said briefly. "The water is polluted. Acid rain, I think."

"It's like a cancer of the land," George said, and was instantly sorry he had. Leigh froze in her tracks, but Mindy, thankfully, had been too busy wrestling with Wolf to hear him.

Stoner didn't bother to answer George. He stopped and swung his hand in a semicircle. "Daisy, if she's here, likes to graze in this area. Don't go deep enough in the woods that you lose sight of the house or the meadow—especially not today."

"Why not?"

His heavy eyebrows arched, setting deep frown lines. "Didn't you hear Johannsen this morning? Wild dogs, and they're hungry."

"Oh. Right."

A clear voice said, "It wasn't dogs. It was weevils."

Now she had to be listening. George felt a chill go up his spine, but he swore pungently and added, "Shut up, Mindy!"

Stoner pointed a rigid finger at him immediately. "Don't talk to your sister like that. You're old enough to know better and I won't tolerate that from you."

George felt like he'd been whipped. His face heated, but he looked at the ground and eyed the fraying toe of his sneaker very closely. "Yes, sir." His blood roared in his ears. Mindy was going to ruin everything, going weird on them again. He saw no sign of hoofprints or horse apples in the grass, but his jaw froze as he thought he saw a tire track in the damp ground beneath the trees. Tires meant cars and he remembered the ember-eyed driver in the dark.

He caught his breath, then clenched his fist and told himself it was probably from a tractor. This had been, after all, a ranch of some sort once. In his paralysis, he heard Stoner move past him and kneel next to Mindy. "What's this about weevils? Are they like your unicorn?"

"Uh-huh."

"No, Mindy, that's not right—" Leigh blurted desperately.

Stoner held his hand up. "Let her talk. She needs to be able to say what she feels. You all do." He stood up. "This summer is going to be a real rough one for all of us, unless we feel like we can say what we want. I know I don't have a rightful place in your lives, but here I am. Say what's on your minds." Then the corner of Stoner's mouth quirked. "Unless, of course, you intend to swear."

He pulled a laundry rope from a loop on his hip, took out a pocketknife, and cut the rope into three good-sized pieces, each six or seven feet long.

George sheepishly took one of the ropes. "You expect me to play cowboy?"

"No. Daisy's not likely to try outrunning us. Walk up to her, pat her on the neck, then just wrap this around her neck and you can lead her." Stoner demonstrated with Wolf, who ended the demonstration with a sloppy kiss across his owner's lined face. Stoner laughed.

The laugh startled George. It was a boyish sound that rang through the sunny meadow. It seemed impossible coming out of someone that craggy and old. He snorted at the oddness of it. His snort sounded like an old goat and Mindy giggled. She rolled in the grass as Wolf bowled her over. Suddenly, the pasture flooded with sunlight and everything seemed a little better.

They didn't find the mare, though George swore he tripped in one of her hoofprints. What they did find were ripening berries, and all of them came home with fingertips and lips stained, and Mindy collapsed for a midday nap on top of the quilt in the loft bedroom.

Stoner fixed them lemonade and tuna salad sandwiches. The tuna salad wasn't as good as Mom's—he hated celery and left it out, so the sandwiches were crunchless, but Leigh reflected that it was pretty good anyway.

She had kind of picked and poked at it, before realizing that nothing would be the way Mom did it for quite a while, and finished her lunch.

After lunch, the man pushed aside his paper plate and rocked back in his chair. He watched them quietly.

George sensed that Stoner had something important to say and gulped down the last of his second sandwich. Under protest, he'd left enough tuna for Mindy to have some when she woke up. His stomach rumbled as though letting him know more foraging was in order.

Stoner tracked an unseen pattern in the tablecloth with a blunt nail. Then he cleared his throat. "Carrie—your mother and I—talked a little bit before you came up. She had me call that counselor you guys all went to see. I want you to know the counselor didn't tell me anything private that you'd told her. Just let me know how counseling works in general. Now, I don't know the three of you very well, but I do know you're going through a really bad time. First your dad and now this. That's why you have to let it out—to say what you feel. I can't understand you if you don't. I don't know if you're comparing me, or if you're feeling homesick, or if you're mad because God let your mother get sick—or what."

Leigh paid a great deal of attention to her empty lemonade glass. She dipped a finger inside the rim and scraped off all the pulp bits and then sucked her finger briefly. Stoner ignored her.

"And that's why you want us to lay off Mindy."

Stoner nodded at George. "That's right. You see, she's invented fantastic characters that she can see in her imagination to represent what she can't see in real life. The unicorn is medicine curing your mother, and I'd say the weevils are probably the cancer. So let her talk about them. She has to work out what she's thinking. She knows that Carrie—ah, Caroline—is dangerously ill. She knows her mother, your mother, could die, though I understand the chemotherapy should be successful. But don't tell her what is and isn't real. She knows—and she's trying to deal with it on her five-year-old level." Stoner tapped the table. "Actually, she's pretty easy to figure out. Your fifteen-year-old level, and your twelve-year-old level—that's got me stumped, so far."

"Me, too," George said, without thinking.

They all began to laugh.

It sounded good, though, until George remembered how quiet the meadow had been until they'd started laughing and shouting before, and that brought the tire tracks back to mind and the driver of the car. He grew very quiet as Leigh began to talk, spilling over, about how hard it was to leave her friends behind. His two sandwiches balled into a very big lump in the pit of his stomach.

After dinner while they watched TV and played on an ancient Nintendo deck, he went upstairs and pulled out some plain paper. Sketching in quick, vigorous lines, he did a pencil version of the face he'd seen through the car window. He looked at it in appraisal. Maned and rugged . . . a werewolf, he thought, but not a movie werewolf. This was like a wolfish, very shrewd, very sharp-faced man. You might almost pass him by if he had his ruff pulled back like a long haircut and he kept his lips skinned down over his teeth. You might almost pass him by unless you looked him in those smoldering eyes. . . . George shuddered. The jolt brought him out of his trancelike observation and he balled the paper up savagely and tossed it in the corner trash can as if he could toss away his discomfort.

On Sunday morning, George pulled on his favorite jeans and discovered they were nearly two inches shorter than he remembered. He sat on the edge of the bed and stared morosely at his ankles and feet sticking out at the bottom. His mom hadn't prepared for that. He'd have to ask Stoner for money to buy a new pair soon. That rankled him. It was all right to visit the man, but to get him to buy them things . . .

A high-pitched argument from across the hall interrupted his thoughts. The girls' voices rose. He took a deep breath to yell at them to shut up, then remembered Stoner and clamped his lips shut tightly. Home, but not home. George got off the bed and crossed the hall.

As he opened their door, Mindy and Leigh were tug-of-warring over the unicorn book. They froze in place and looked at him in surprise. Leigh's light-colored hair stuck out everywhere, but George was more shocked by Mindy's appearance, still pale, with purple shadows lingering under her eyes.

He lowered his voice to a vicious whisper. "What's going on here?"

"She wants to take that thing to the Johannsens, and I won't let her!"

"But I have to! I have to keep it warm and . . . and in the light . . . and with me," Mindy sputtered. Her eyes had that wide, frightened Bambi look in them again.

George sighed. Leigh had that stubborn I'll-jump-off-a-cliff-first look written all over her face. He leaned against the doorframe. Why couldn't both he and Leigh be patient with Mindy at the same time?

"Listen, Min—we're going to a real farm. The Johannsens have lots of kids . . . one or two your age. We're going to be helping them milk, and feed the chickens, and all sorts of things. You'll lose Rosebud if you take it with you! We're going to be awfully busy, and then there's the picnic. Okay?"

Mindy waited until Leigh relaxed, then snatched the book back. She turned to face George as she hugged it close. "I can't put it up."

"Okay, fine." George straightened up, glancing around the room. Light from the shuttered window streamed inward, in broken lines. It pooled on the floor. "Here. Put the book right there. Just like a cat curling up in the sunlight."

Mindy looked dubious.

"Go on. Try it."

She went to the sunbeam and put down the book. Nothing happened, though her body tensed as though she thought it might. Leigh gave George an odd look and he shrugged. Then Mindy gave a tight smile.

"Guess it'll be all right."

"Put on your shoes and socks, then. I'll go tell Dave we're almost ready." George shut the door behind him and made for the stairs, shaking his head. He'd chalked up his nightmares to nerves, but Mindy didn't look as if she'd ever settle down.

The doorbell rang and he froze at the top of the stairs as Stoner crossed the immense living room to answer it. For half a second, George wondered if red-eyed beasts rang doorbells.

Two men in three-piece suits stood on the front stoop as Stoner pulled the door open. George faded back a little at the top of the stairs. Something about Stoner's stance telegraphed hostility all the way up to George. He didn't want Stoner to know he stood up there, listening.

"Dave Stoner?"

"Yes."

"Sorry to bother you at home on a Sunday, but . . ."

"That's all right. What can I do for you?" The words were courteous enough, but Stoner didn't move back to let the men in.

"We represent a certain, ah, developer—"

"Let me guess. I have a pretty good idea where you're coming from," Stoner said. "River Valley."

One of the men flushed a little, but the other cleared his throat and moved forward, across the doorjamb. "We'd like a moment of your time."

Stoner looked at his watch. He didn't budge. He and

the intruder were nearly nose to nose as he answered, "That's about all the time I have. I have an appointment in a few moments."

George heard Mindy and Leigh rustle behind him. He waved them back down the hallway. For once, they responded quickly and quietly. He found he'd been holding his breath.

"Then we'll make it quick, Stoner. Our employer thinks you've made a mountain out of a molehill. Spirit Lake is a promising property."

"What are you suggesting?" Stoner's voice rumbled ominously, the way thunder does after lightning.

"We'd like to suggest that your test results are wrong, and that your reasons for not selling to River Valley aren't valid."

"Alter my results? Sell out to you so you can build vacation homes on a dying lake? What do you have in mind, forcing me to sell out like you did most of downtown? Maybe a racial-ethnic thing like you tried to do to Sun Ling at the gallery?"

The two men shifted weight uneasily.

Stoner's back tensed, threatening to rip the worn cotton shirt. "Even if the lake weren't polluted, I wouldn't sell to you. Those were sacred grounds once. It deserves more than yuppies and water-ski boats. And I'm not so sure River Valley isn't responsible for some of the problem. Maybe you've been doing some dumping upstream? Driving down the property value a little?" They said nothing. The door trembled in Stoner's grip. "Get out," he said, finally. "Get out and don't come back."

"You can't prove anything, of course," one of the men said. "But if you were to make accusations, I must warn you . . . living in the woods like this . . . you must have quite a fire hazard. Yes, I'd say a fire could cause you a lot of pain and grief."

"Get out!" Stoner roared, and the two men moved,

quickly. He slammed the door shut, and the house reverberated.

George stood quietly until he could tell that Stoner had recovered. He cleared his throat and went back to get the girls.

Mindy slid a hand inside his. She looked up, her round face even more troubled.

George sighed. Nothing about this summer was going to be easy.

FOUR

STONER SET THE BRAKE AS THE VEhicle rolled into the Johannsen driveway. The kids boiled out of the doors as he said, "Don't worry about letting Wolf go. He knows this place."

But Wolf sat still in the backseat, his ears pricked, eyes uncannily alive in his black-and-silver face. Stoner looked back to him, mildly surprised. "Go on, Wolf."

George waited, poised in all his lankiness, hanging on the car door. Wolf hesitated a second longer, then got out. As he sniffed the familiar ground, his hackles went up a little. Stoner got out of the car and put his hand down to the dog's back and rubbed it, feeling the tension. That wasn't like Wolf—he knew the Johannsen spread well, and loved running here. It was hard to keep him out of the woods.

George yelled, "C'mon, Wolf!" as his sisters sprinted away from them to be engulfed by four excited girls. An aloof, boyish-looking shadow awaited George behind the rear porch. The dog made up his mind and went with George then, as Tom Johannsen added a coaxing whistle.

Stoner rubbed the back of his neck. Then he

smelled the aroma of a Sunday pot of coffee from the kitchen window and, with a sigh, went in to visit.

Tom arched a knowing eyebrow and stuck out a hand as George and the dog approached. "I'm Tom," he said. He was shorter than George, and stockier, but about the same age. He shrugged to the girls. "Don't let my sisters drive you crazy."

George grinned. Four strawberry blonds bounced around Mindy and Leigh. The tallest of them glanced shyly his way, and he was struck by her glowing Swedish good looks. He swallowed, then the girl looked away, and Tom jabbed him in the ribs. "Who—who's that?"

"Astrid. She's fifteen." Tom grimaced.

The girl looked George's way again, then leaned down and said something to Leigh. His sister's laughter pealed out and George felt his face flush. To take the attention off himself, George asked, "Who are the others?"

"Oh, these are my twin sisters Kim and Melanie, and the other one there, that's Sandy."

The twins engulfed Mindy in their whirlwind of chatter.

The noise and smell of the Johannsen spread bombarded George as they went to the barn. A battered yellow tomcat rubbed against his ankle, spat at Wolf, and went to lie down in the sun. Chickens clucked and pecked. He heard other sounds he couldn't quite identify, but he smelled the pungent odor of the farmyard. He watched as Astrid drifted ahead of his sister. The one named Sandy caught up and he could hear their voices.

Sandy stayed with her. "We saved feeding the animals until you got here. Mom said you'd think it was fun. It is—the first couple of times. When you've gotta get up at five-thirty and there's frost out here, well, that's different." She pulled open the weather-beaten gray door of the barn.

Mindy and the twins were already spreading chicken feed. They had to convince Mindy not to hug the chickens. The girls and fowl ran in and out of the sunlit doorway, and dust motes floated like golden particles in the air. Sandy pulled out a sack. "This is for the rabbits."

"Rabbits?"

"Yeah, and then there's bottles for the lambs and goats, and we've got two calves, too." Sandy smiled back. "But no horses. Dad said you liked horses."

Leigh nodded as she took the battered tin scoop of rabbit pellets.

"Then we've got good news—Daisy's around here somewhere. Dad saw her this morning, and Micah—that's the guy who owns her—Dad called him up, and he said you could have her for the summer if you could catch her."

Astrid drifted into the barn with all of her fifteen-year-old dignity and added softly, "But the animals have got to be taken care of first, before we go looking. Dad also said." She brushed Nordic blond hair from her temple, discreetly eyeing George and her brother.

Sandy shrugged. She led Leigh to the rabbit hutches leaning in the shade of the barn. They stood on stilts, and droppings rained upon tin pans below them on the ground. Sandy spied them. "Almost enough for another gunny sack."

Leigh shook out her scoop of pellets and wrinkled her nose. "You have to clean that up?"

"Hey—rabbit pellets make great fertilizer. The principal at school buys 'em from me all the time. Says they're great for her roses. I make three bucks a bag—almost enough to pay for the feed."

Leigh giggled. "They don't look much different going in than coming out!"

Sandy pulled large plastic baby bottles out of the beaten-up refrigerator that wheezed and cranked unhappily in a shadowed corner. At the sound of the door's squeak, two pink-and-white-and-black noses immediately poked out from stall doors and the calves began to fuss.

Mindy sat down in the stall, unmindful of the trampled straw, as Sandy and the twins gave her a bottle and a calf. Her big brown eyes, so like those of the baby she fed, reflected a complete and utter peace. George came in and leaned over the side of the stall.

"You'll have to watch it. We'll never get her home now. She's going to want to be a farmer."

Tom gave a crooked smile. "You get used to it. That's why we're only 'gentlemen ranchers.' Dad makes his real living in the city."

Not George's New York City, but a far enough drive. "What's he do?"

"He's a computer programmer."

"That's quite a ways."

Tom nodded and unhooked the next stall as his sister handed him a bottle and a rambunctious baby goat butted him in the leg. "Dad drives in on Tuesday and stays overnight two nights, then comes home late Thursdays. He says he's got the best of both worlds. My mom worries in the winter when the weather's bad, but he usually doesn't leave the city then. It's worked out." He handed the bottle to George, with a kid goat firmly fastened onto it. "Hold on. These babies are stronger than they look!"

"I know. We've got two at Stoner's."

George kept the bottle firmly grasped as the goat played tug-of-war on the heavy-duty nipple. It stood on its hind legs, front hooves balanced on his legs, so determined to drink that George could barely hold onto the bottle.

A puzzled expression passed over Tom's face. He said, "Stoner told my dad you were into computers and stuff."

"Yeah. I was signed up to go to a local college this summer and take animation courses. It was a neat program. But then this happened." George shrugged. He didn't want the other boy feeling sorry for him.

"The girls like this kind of stuff." Tom gave a chuff, sounding a little like Wolf. "Want to see my computer? Dad pieced it together. I've got a drawing program, color monitor, it's 386-chipped—"

George wrestled with the kid to take the bottle away. It gave a forlorn bleat. "Think we could? I can only take so much of this petting-zoo stuff."

Tom took the bottle from him with a grin and threw it to one of his sisters. "We're outta here," he said. "Follow me."

They hiked up the back stairs. The sound of a printer at work, punctuated by keyboarding, filled the upper story. Tom pointed with his chin. "That's Dad's office. He's got a better system, but the company provided that. Mine was salvaged out of the repair bin. He put it together himself. We bought the printer with my Christmas money."

He led George into a room jumbled with the life of a teen. The sloping roof and mullioned windows looked out over the back pasture and barn. Against one wall, a concrete-block-and-board bookcase held the computer system. George felt his palms itch. He watched as Tom fished a pile of old jeans off the chair, sat down, and booted up. He pointed to a tall stool.

"Plant your butt."

"Don't mind if I do." Tom's easy familiarity made George feel comfortable. He edged close to see what the computer could do.

Tom's fingers flew over the keys. As he pulled up his drawing program from the hard disk, he said, "Heard you were in a bad accident last year."

George's stomach went cold, as though he'd swallowed ice. "Yeah," he got out. "It killed my dad."

"I heard you don't remember much about it."

"No." Then George thought he'd answered too quickly. "No, I don't. I got hit in the head. The doctors say it happens all the time with car accidents. You don't remember anything but waking up in the hospital. I woke up first in the ER, but it was all hazy. They didn't tell me my dad was dead until after the funeral."

"Bummer," Tom said.

George didn't answer. He missed his father, but he didn't. He didn't miss the raging anger, the sarcasm, the perfectionism. He caught sight of the program coming up as Tom put a light pen in his hand. "Let's see what you can do," the Johannsen boy challenged.

George put the pen to the screen and began quickly to sketch out his imagined vision of the old white mare they'd come looking for. Tom let out a low whistle as the sketch took shape.

"That's good," he said.

Deep in concentration, George answered absently, "I know." He blinked and looked up. "Now what can we do with it?"

Tom grinned. "Watch."

Dave looked out the kitchen window and watched the silhouettes of the children in the barn. The happy shouts and animal noises drifted through the screened door.

Inga Johannsen leaned over him to pour a second cup of coffee. She was a tall, raw-boned woman, her pale complexion perpetually sunburned, and her light blond hair pulled back into a ponytail. "Happy sounds, aren't they?"

He tapped his fingers on the now too hot cup. "Yes."

She sat down beside him. "Doesn't it make you wonder what it would be like if they were yours?"

In surprise, he looked at Inga. "Boy. You get right into it, don't you?"

The woman laughed. She was six years older than Stoner, settling comfortably into middle age, and there were ample smile lines about her pale blue eyes. "We're too close neighbors to waste time, eh? But don't you wonder?"

He looked out and saw Leigh's coltish body framed by the open windows, ambulating through the barn. "I haven't had a chance yet—they just got here. But, yeah, I guess I might wonder."

"Any chance the boy's—"

"Mine? Not a one. Carrie and I were divorced several years when she married and then had George." Dave cleared his throat and retreated to the safer, if hotter, coffee. Inga seemed to sense the change in conversation, for she said nothing further, but watched fondly out the back door. He asked, "How come the animals aren't in the pasture? It's a beautiful day."

"Eric's worried about those wild dogs. He's told Tom and Astrid not to wander off. The gang wants to go looking for Daisy before lunch, and I told them they could go as soon as the chores were done."

"Where is Eric, anyway?"

Inga looked toward the ceiling. "Upstairs."

Faintly, then, Dave could hear the tic-tac of computer keys. "How's he doing? He seemed upset about the killings."

"Fine." Inga took a swallow of coffee and savored it. "He's right, though, Dave. Those wild dogs did some savage work."

"I'll keep my eyes peeled this week."

"Take your shotgun. There's enough of them to pull a man down, from the looks of it."

He held up both hands. "Peace, Inga!"

She laughed. "I know, you can take care of yourself." She looked out the window again. She pointed at the boys, who had emerged from the back of the house. They seemed deep in conversation. Then she frowned. "What's Wolf doing out there?"

The barn burst open, and the girls poured out. He caught a glimpse of dark-haired Mindy being raced to the back pasture by the twin Johannsens. Leigh and Sandy followed.

He stood up. "The girls are going after Daisy."

Inga stood up, too, and went to the screen door, but she was looking in a different direction. "Dave, I think Wolf's scented something." Her voice went up a tiny bit.

The silver-and-black dog circled the barn, his nose to the ground. He ignored Dave's whistle. The hackles stayed up on his back until he looked to the woods beyond the far pastures. For a moment Stoner thought the dog watched the children, but then he bared his teeth and threw back his head. An eerie howl wrenched out of the dog's throat.

Dave went cold. He slapped the back of Inga's hand. "Get Eric. Tell him to bring his shotgun!" He bolted out of the screen door after Wolf.

The children had already run so far that the forest cast shadows across their retreating forms. He could barely see them. As he shouted for Wolf, the dog skittered to a halt and waited for him.

White fangs glistened as the dog swung his muzzle toward his master. Dave grabbed the ruff of his neck and Wolf gave a low growl. *Something* was out there, all right—and the kids were headed straight for it!

He shoved the dog. "Go get 'em, boy!" As Wolf took off in a streak, he cupped his hands, yelling, but knew the children couldn't hear him. As an icy sweat sheeted his forehead, he broke into his own run. The screen door banged and he knew Eric Johannsen was on his heels.

Wind and sun in her face, Leigh surged to the front, leaving the others behind except for a determined Sandy, who kept pace with her. The green grasses bent and bruised under her sneakered feet. Shadows from lone trees whipped across her path. Behind them, Astrid yelled, "You can't sneak up on a horse that way!" Panting thinned out her protest and Leigh grinned.

The wind bit at her exposed teeth. She knew where a horse would be. As she tossed her head, coltlike, she knew that the shadows of the forest would hide her. Give her sweet grass to eat, and deep ponds to water at. Sandy threw her a desperate look, fair face pinked with effort, and slowly dropped back until Leigh raced in front, all alone.

She saw a stile over the fencing, as the pastureland came to an abrupt end, ringed by forest. She thundered over the weathered steps and leapt off the other side. Instantly, she plunged into a chill and different land. The forest swallowed her. Behind her, she could hear the others clambering over the stile. Mindy let out a high sound of fear. Comforting voices drowned her out.

Still smiling, Leigh slowed a little and turned her face to the deepest part of the woods, expectant.

"Hey, Leigh! Slow up!"

She dropped back a little more. Besides, she didn't want to get lost.

Something snagged at the cuff of Leigh's pants and she stumbled. She pulled herself upright, but not before she nearly fell face first into the bloody thicket.

Her stomach pitched. Leigh let out a tiny sound and pivoted around, and threw herself at Sandy, to keep her away. The bloodied remains of a deer lay behind her. She gasped. "Get Mindy!"

The others swerved away from her. George hugged Mindy as he caught up, and Tom and he traded looks. "What's wrong?"

Leigh shook her head, unable to answer. She put her hand to her mouth unsuccessfully, turned, and vomited into the needle-covered ground.

As Astrid and Sandy helped her, Tom solemnly went to look at the kill. With his knife, he cut down extra branches to cover the site while Mindy whined in the background, "I wanna see! What is it?"

The girls kicked dirt and pine needles over Leigh's disgrace. Sandy handed her a patch of moss. Not real green or moist, she thought, as it scratched her lips, but something to wipe her face on, anyway.

Tom said, "Dad's going to have to know about this. I think we'd better forget about Daisy and get back to the house."

Leigh shivered. Something was out here in these woods . . . something that killed. Something horrible.

A branch crackled. Sandy didn't seem to hear it, but Leigh did. She swung her face to meet the sound.

Something white disappeared beyond her seeing. She shrugged out of Sandy's hold. "What was that?"

"What was what?"

George and Tom straightened. "If you saw something, then we'd better get out of here now."

Leigh took a few steps closer. She saw the scrap of white again, almost a misty fineness, to the east. "There it is!"

Astrid and Sandy frowned and shook their heads. Leigh jogged after it. "It's the mare, I know it is!"

Behind her, George shouted, "Come back!" And from very far away, she thought she heard Stoner's voice. But it didn't make any difference. It was the mare, she knew it, and now she had to find it, to save it from the killer beast in the forest.

Leigh bolted. Branches snapped back in her face. She drew closer . . . the misty white outline solidified. It was a horse! The mare stopped, looked at her, then shook her head, mane falling over her like sea foam. She was close-crouped, and thick through the arched neck, like a Lippizaner, one of those dancing white horses from Vienna.

Leigh called to her. "Come here, beauty! Come here!"

The creature threw back her head in skittish alarm and turned to bolt deeper into the woods.

Leigh threw herself after the beast, grabbing for a handful of the thick, cascading mane—

—and with a chill, she realized her hand had passed right through the animal's form.

FIVE

MINDY WAS RELIEVED TO FIND her unicorn book still in a puddle of light from the window when they got back home. Disgruntled at George and Leigh for not letting her in on the mystery—they'd been talking in hushed tones ever since Stoner found them in the woods and he and Mr. Johannsen had looked at the dead deer—she scooped up Rosebud and retreated to the bed.

Leigh closed the shutters and took off Mindy's shoes and pulled the fraying quilt over her. "Why don't you rest for a couple of minutes. We've got to feed our own goats again."

Mindy stared at her a minute, then realized she was awfully sleepy. She nodded and scrunched down into the bed.

Stoner had taken Wolf and gone to check out the boundaries of his pastureland, so it was the first time Leigh and George had had a chance to talk alone.

George swung open the shed door. The overwhelming pungency of the goats hit him and he realized he would have to shovel out the stalls and spread fresh straw in the morning. Monday . . . one of his first days out of school, and he was going to spend it in manure. Tom Johannsen was right. Farm animals were a lot cuter when they belonged to someone else.

It was late. They'd had so much for lunch at the Johannsens' that he knew he wasn't going to want any dinner—maybe hot chocolate and toast. The shadows were cast long and low over the yard. Leigh carried the baby bottles and fed both goats at once, while he hooked his elbows over the stall door and watched her.

"Well?" he said over the noisy slurping of the kids.

"Well, what?"

"When are you going to tell me what it was that made you screech like a banshee?"

Leigh felt her face get hot. "Something scared me."

"I know that. What? You didn't even scream when you saw the carcass."

"You're going to tease me."

George lifted his chin. "I'm going to throw you in a pile of goat droppings if you don't tell me."

Leigh paused, struck by his language, then said, "I saw something. I was sure it was the old mare. It—it was something white, so I ran after it and caught up with it."

"And was it old Daisy?"

"I . . . don't know. She was all tangled in the pine branches and then she kind of plunged to leave, so I jumped her."

"And?"

"My hand went right through her."

Incredulity shot through George's face. Then he snorted. "Come on, Leigh. What do you take me for? Telling me ghost stories."

"Honest to God, George! My hand went right through the horse! That's what made me scream."

George opened his mouth to protest being made a fool of again, and stopped. Something had definitely unnerved Leigh—she wasn't the screaming type. And whatever it was, he could see the haunting fright still in her eyes. He shrugged. "Maybe it was a patch of sunlight."

"*George*."

He stiffened. Leigh could be an awful lot like their mother. "All right. I believe you. Why don't you tell Stoner about it?"

"Are you kidding? He came after us with a gun."

"A shotgun. And that was Mr. Johannsen, not Stoner. And it was because of Wolf acting so funny. And we did find that deer all torn up."

"And that's another thing." But if Leigh had another thought, she didn't finish it. One of the kids, the black-and-white one, pulled so hard the nipple came off the bottle and milk spurted everywhere.

George tackled the kid to keep it from swallowing the piece of rubber as Leigh squealed and tried to right the bottle. He took over feeding the greedy beast as she finished with the soft brown one.

When he was done, the goat lay asleep across his legs. He pulled the empty bottle from slack lips and looked at Leigh, who cuddled a like bundle. "Why don't you want to tell Stoner?" he repeated.

"Because all this stuff has happened since we got here, and Mindy and her weevils and all. We've got to live here for three months, remember? I don't want him thinking we're jinxed."

George shuddered when Leigh said, "Isn't that Mindy?"

In the quiet of the shed, he could almost hear a faraway wail. He bolted up, dumping the kid from his lap.

As they approached the house, it was nearly dusk. The wind had picked up and roared through the forest's edge like the tide of angry ocean. Mindy's crying could barely be heard. He pulled at the door. The knob refused to turn in his hand.

"Damn! It's locked."

"I didn't do it," Leigh countered before he could accuse her. She turned on her heel and ran around to the front.

When George caught up with her, she was pounding on the front door, yelling, "Mindy! Let us in!"

Their sister's frightened crying continued, but she did nothing to let them in. "We're locked out," Leigh muttered, showing her gift for the obvious.

A pinecone rolled off the roof and dropped near them. George craned his head. "Something's up there."

"Can't be. It's just the wind."

George shivered. He looked up again, afraid of what he might see. "No," he answered slowly. "I think something's up there."

Leigh paused. A scrunch reached them. She turned to look at George, her eyes very wide.

He bent and picked up a very large stone from the border that ringed the empty flower beds near the doorway. He tossed it up and down in his palm, calculating its weight for a proper throw.

It was nearly dark now. Mindy's wailing had broken into loud sobs. Leigh rubbed her bare arms.

They both heard it at once, a thump, and then the rush of something over the dirt and grass and gravel toward them from around the corner of the house. George cocked his arm, rock in hand.

Wolf gave a loud bark and jumped at them, his tail waving. George dropped the rock guiltily as Stoner came around the corner. "You left the goat shed open."

"I—we're sorry," Leigh said. "We're locked out. Mindy's scared."

"Locked out?"

"She's in there alone," George offered.

Stoner opened the front door quickly and stood back as Leigh forced her slender body through and took the stairs two at a time.

The three of them burst into the loft bedroom almost together. Mindy sat in the closet, her pale face bent over her teddy and her book, her dark brown hair practically standing on end.

Leigh took her in her arms. "What is it? Why'd you lock us out? Why didn't you let us in?"

Mindy stopped crying momentarily, then said, "I didn't think it was you."

Stoner knelt down and reached out, smoothing down the girl's hair. "Did you have a nightmare?"

"A weevil tried to get me. It was at the window. I couldn't see it because the shutters were closed, but it scratched."

George and Leigh looked at each other.

"I heard something on the roof," the boy said slowly. He felt his blood drain and knew his freckles must be standing out.

Stoner looked to the shuttered window. "Squirrels, probably."

"No," gulped their sister. "It was a weevil! And it wants Mommy, too. It told me so."

Stoner got up. His kneecap popped slightly as he did so, reminding George of the man's age. The man ran a hand through graying hair, then reached for the shutters and threw them open.

"Nothing's out there, sweetie," he said, then stared as George gasped.

Deep gouges scored the glass. Not scratches, but grooves, five of them, in a pattern that a clawed paw might have made.

They all stared as Mindy pointed triumphantly and George asked, "What kind of squirrel can do *that?*"

SIX

AT BEDTIME, DAVE STATIONED WOLF in the upstairs hallway. The dog lay down, a bit baffled, for his bed was in the kitchen. "Stay," Stoner ordered. Wolf finally put his muzzle on his paws as Dave ordered him to. His eyes reflected eerily green as the last light went out. George could see him blink in the darkness, before he shrugged into his covers. Sleep eluded him, so he did as he always did . . . he drew himself a dream. On a plain white sheet of paper as pure as a snowfield, he began to sketch out a picture of comfort for himself and, as it always did, the picture pulled him in until it became a dream. For a while, the dream was good.

George thrashed under the covers of his bed. He was locked out of the boys' locker room again, and his shower towel refused to stay rolled about his waist. As sweat beaded his forehead, he huddled closer and his dream changed to more mundane things.

He was in the woods behind Johannsen's farm again, dressed as he had been, shirt, too-short jeans, hole-eaten sneakers. But the summer sun that had dappled through the trees was gone. It was dark and chill. He looked up, wondering if rain clouds closed in overhead, but this was different, leaden, molten, almost alive. He shivered. Then it occurred to George that he was dreaming. He shrugged defiantly, trying to throw off the image, and brushed the back of his hand over his forehead. A crackling of needles filled the air and he froze.

The trees dipped branches about him. Some were needled, some with leaves like small coins fluttering in the wind, some with leaves sharp-pointed and bowed, boats that would sail upon the breeze when they fell in the autumn.

He heard the crackle again, and a stubborn, determined voice. "Rats!"

"Mindy? Is that you?" George pushed forward again. One of the coin-leaved trees caught him up, the branch whipping into his face. George caught it with a grunt. The sting lashed across his palm, but better his hand than his eyes. He put his hand to his lips and sucked at the lash. "Now I know what Hansel and Gretel felt like," he muttered. More loudly, he called out, "Mindy, is that you?"

The shrubbery in front of him rustled ferociously, and a pale face edged in sable peered out. "George? But this is my dream!"

"What are you doing out here?"

"I lost my book."

He groaned. For two cents, he'd burn the damn thing this time. Even if it was a work of art. "Come on, we've got to get back."

Mindy looked at his hand as if he'd sprouted an alien tentacle. "How do I know it's you?"

"How long have you been out here, anyway?" George scowled and then Mindy giggled.

"It's you. You're getting cranky, like Mom says you always do."

He scuffed a shoe into the dirt. "Are you coming or not?"

"As soon as I find my book." Mindy tilted her head. "Will you help?"

With a groan, he answered, "Don't I always?" and followed after her into the heart of the forest deep. He heard wind, smelled pine sap, brushed through needled branches, felt them snap back in his face. He thought of virtual-reality computer programming and wondered what was happening to him.

The green waves of the woods swallowed them whole, drawing them closer and closer to a deep forest that let no light through it. As George drew near, he reached out and caught Mindy by the sleeve of her sweater. As he pinched it, the thought ran through his head that this sweater had once been Leigh's. He wondered when Mindy had inherited it. Time seemed to run like a slow molasses river.

"I want Rosebud!" Mindy protested.

"Come back here." His heart thumped heavily in his chest. "I don't like this, Mindy. Stay with me."

She ceased fighting him and backed toward him. She pointed at the forest heart. "What's that?"

A massive hillock sat in the middle of a dark and fetid glen, ringed by slimy-looking toadstools. The trees and underbrush had retreated from the knoll, but their branches had gone black and moist, as if diseased. George shivered. It smelled bad. It *looked* bad.

"I don't know. Look, your book can't be here . . . we've never been here before. Let's go back."

"But the weevils took it. The weevils took it and brought it here, I know they did."

Ice thrilled through George. He swallowed hard. As he looked toward the black hillock, two slits opened, as though the mass were a gigantic head dismembered and set on the ground, asleep in the woods, and they had awakened it. The eye slits smoldered red. The air rumbled as the thing said, "Come here."

Its wolflike jaws opened wider, and he glimpsed the

crimson embers of its maw, spiked by ivory fangs. Two tufted ears pricked up. "Do they know, George? Do they know who was driving yet, George? Come closer."

Mindy squeaked out, "It's the king of weevils!"

George reached down and scooped her up, threw her over his shoulder, turned face, and *ran*.

Branches ripped heedlessly at them. Mindy squeaked with every jolting step he took and he muttered a litany to calm her, "I'm sorry, I'm sorry, I'm sorry." But he never slowed. He'd thought once of going out for the track team, being good at sprints and hurdles, and now he put his dream to the test.

Something sprang at his elbow with a growl. George saw its ruddy eyes. A man-beast. Hot, rank breath scorched his face. It tore at his sleeve and the fabric gave way. George let a branch whip past him. It caught the beast. It let out a shrill yelp and George sprang away as Mindy began to cry.

He tore through the woods. The trees that had hindered his entrance now bowed to let him past. The pine needles crushed beneath his flying feet, and he jumped shrubs that grew higher than his belt buckle, and swore they ducked under his sneakers.

Mindy's low sobs quieted as they spotted the edge of the sunlight, where the forest gave way to pastureland. "They don't like sun," she gasped to George.

"We're almost there." His breath sobbed in his chest like raw flames. His shoulders ached with Mindy's weight.

Behind them, something snarled.

George threw himself across the last patch of forestland as Mindy let out a shrill scream.

In the night, two children gasped together. Leigh sat bolt upright in the bed and grabbed for Mindy, as George's harsh voice echoed across the hall. Her heart thumped like a drum as Mindy clutched at her.

Her little sister breathed, then shuddered and drew closer.

Leigh stroked her hair. "It was just a bad dream. Okay?" Her eyes were swollen and tender with sleep, and she felt tired and achy all over. How could Mom stand getting up at night all the time? She pushed Mindy back onto the pillows. "Come on, go back to sleep."

Mindy scrubbed at one eye. "I had a dream and George was in it and weevils, too, and—"

Leigh hit her with the pillow. "Go to sleep! Or I'll make you sleep downstairs on the couch."

Her sister's ghostly face went pink with surprise. Her little round mouth opened and shut several times, then she said, "I'm telling Mr. Stoner on you."

"Go right ahead. He's right next door trying to sleep, too."

"I will." Mindy blinked. "In the morning." She tucked her chin in under the blankets. "Can I still sleep with you?"

Leigh sighed. "*Yes.* Now shut up, will you?" As she scrunched back down, Mindy turned on her side and backed up a little, so that she fit into the curve of Leigh's body.

In a few moments, Mindy's breathing deepened into a soft purr, and Leigh knew she was asleep again. She lay in the warm darkness and wondered what had made George yell, too. As she searched for a return to sleep, she heard the sounds of the house at night. And in them, something moved restlessly.

Her heart skipped a beat as she listened, afraid. Then she identified the sounds as Stoner on the other side of the wall, tossing and groaning on the stiff old couch.

Everybody, she thought, was having bad dreams tonight.

Dave Stoner slept scared that night, for the first time in twenty years. He'd slept alone, sick, drunk, tired, disgusted, frustrated, crying, but not scared. At least, not when he laid his head down. Sometimes the fear came later.

But he hadn't gone to sleep afraid since he'd left Nam, after almost two years of going to sleep nightly afraid. Afraid he wouldn't wake up in the morning, or afraid when he did wake up, he'd find himself in enemy hands. Those things came back to him now and then. He couldn't shake them.

Today, now, was supposed to be different. He'd been careful not to let the children see his fear. He'd exchanged the window pane for a storm window rescued from oblivion in the attic, and the double thickness of glass seemed to reassure Mindy. They'd had hot chocolate, toast, and cheese omelets, huddled together and watched TV—Mom's favorite Sunday night whodunit, and then gone to bed. Subdued. Quiet. Pale. Even George's thin veneer of confidence was vanishing.

Dave lay on his battered den couch, put his hands under his head, and looked at the ceiling for a long time. His heart raced even though he tried to calm it. He had an early morning and a room addition to finish framing. And just when he'd almost calmed himself to sleep, his mind jolted back.

What had he gotten himself into, taking Carrie's kids for the summer? What personal demons had they brought with them . . . they, shadows of the life he might have had with Carrie if it hadn't been for the war? He couldn't have refused Carrie anything she'd asked of him, but he wished it hadn't been this.

Something had spooked Wolf at the Johannsen farm. And whatever it was that had killed the deer, it had done a messy, torturous job of it. Eric had taken what was left of the carcass into town and left it at the vet's, to see if they could determine from the bite marks if it had been wild dogs, or what.

Or what. What had made those gouges in the glass

trying to get in at Mindy? And if he and Wolf hadn't come back when they did, would it have gone after George and Leigh, locked out of the house?

He shuddered and closed his eyes against the darkness, willing himself not to think, and slipped away into fearful sleep.

Dave Stoner woke up. Sweat poured from his body. The sheet tangled about him like a boa constrictor and his pulse thundered through his temples. Night terrors. He couldn't remember what he'd dreamed, only that he felt like bolting through the darkness away from it.

He took a deep, cutting breath. It was like fighting the war all over again.

Dave put a shaking hand to his forehead to wipe it dry, but his fingers trembled violently. Instead, he dipped his face down and scrubbed the edge of the sheet over it. After he'd lost Carrie, nightmares so real and disturbing he feared to sleep had been frequent. Eventually, they'd gone. Now, the children were here with fresh terrors of their own and Dave found the dreams he'd thought buried coming up again. To steady his nerves, Stoner reached out for a seldom used pipe, a lighter, and a small can of pipe tobacco that rested on the sagging bookshelf near the couch.

A muffled knock came at the den door. He could hear George clear his throat awkwardly and say, "Stoner?"

Dave sat up on the couch. "Come on in."

The boy stood in the door. He looked tall and off-balance somehow. "I—um, I'm sorry I woke you."

"I was awake already." Stoner ran his hand through his hair, then cradled his pipe and lit it carefully.

"I know . . . I mean, I'm sorry about yelling."

Stoner's eyebrows went up. "Sit down, George. Did you yell? I didn't hear you."

George sat on the old chair's edge. "You didn't? I

thought the whole world heard me. I woke Leigh and Mindy."

The pipe let out a satisfying, aromatic puff of smoke. In the graying light of the room, the man saw the fright of the boy. "What can I do for you? Tonight seems to be a bad night for sleeping."

"You, too, huh?" George's eyes took in the crumpled blanket and sheet. "What did you dream about?"

"I usually don't remember the nightmares. Vietnam, I suppose."

"You don't remember?"

Stoner smiled grimly around the stem of the pipe. "It's an intense kind of nightmare. The mind reacts, but blacks it out."

"Oh." George grimaced. "I remember mine."

Stoner waited.

George gripped the curved arms of the chair, then lifted his right hand in surprise and eyed his palm in surprise. He rubbed it reflectively with his left thumb. "Can, ah . . . can two people have the same dream?"

Stoner wondered what it was the boy really wanted to say. He took the pipe out of his lips and held it, the bowl warming his fingers slightly. "I don't think so. But I'm no expert. Why?"

"Because I think Mindy was in mine. And there were things in the forest . . . like werewolves . . . after us. She called them weevils. And normally I wouldn't think about it except—" George looked away, at the wall, toward where the girls' shuttered window would be, and they both thought of the etchings in the glass.

The best way, Stoner thought, to get through this was to shed some light on it. Like the shadowy corner that always scares kids at night. "Ever see a weevil?"

"I don't think so."

"But Mindy has?"

George shrugged.

"Let's ask her." Stoner pulled his jeans off the end of the couch and stood up, slipping them on. With George in tow, he knocked on the girls' door. Leigh's voice was not all that sleepy when she said, "Come in," and he wondered if she'd been listening to them talk.

She shook Mindy as Stoner turned on the light. Mindy blinked and yawned. Then she brightened. "Hi, George! Were you scared too? Boy, I was."

George looked at the floor as though he'd rather be somewhere else.

Stoner came to the edge of the bed and sat on it. The old mattress sagged under his weight. "Would you mind talking about it?"

"No! I wanted to, but Leigh hit me with the pillow and told me to go back to sleep, only I was scared—"

She ran out of breath as Leigh said, "I did not."

Stoner shushed Leigh.

Mindy told Stoner in a rush of words about being summoned into a dark forest, looking for her stolen book, meeting George, and then seeing this big wolflike head that looked at them and wanted them to come closer so it could eat them, probably, then George picked her up and they ran away.

Stoner looked at George. "That about it?"

The boy nodded. He looked squarely at the man then. "It's not possible, is it?"

Stoner looked back at Mindy. Leigh reached over and combed a long section of sable hair from her sister's face. "Can you describe what a weevil looks like?"

"Sure. And I can show you, too. There's pictures in my book."

"Uh-uh." George was suddenly sure of himself. "There's nothing like that in the Rosebud book."

Leigh chimed in, "George was going to send the book to a publisher, to sell it, only Mindy wouldn't let him."

But Mindy had already squeezed past Stoner and out

of bed. She yanked the closet door open where the book lay in a blaze of light.

Leigh let out an indignant sound. "I told you to turn the closet light off."

"I can't do that. Weevils like the dark." She thumped back onto the bed, dropping the book in Stoner's lap.

As he opened it, the children crowded close around him. He became aware that the wind whistled through the trees outside, and that the muted light of the bedroom seemed to grow dimmer.

He opened a page. Handwriting, beautifully lettered and illuminated, stared back at him: *Rosebud, the Children's Unicorn.*

He turned another page. These were the images he'd seen two nights ago when he'd picked the children up. Then another page crinkled under his fingertips.

Impatiently, Mindy seized the book. "Here!" she said triumphantly and jabbed it back at him.

Two man-wolf beings menaced the white unicorn. Their lines, crude and dark, dominated the page. The unicorn wore a look of terror. Red eyes glowed in evil triumph.

"Those are weevils!" Mindy crowed, even as George choked.

"Those pages were never in there before!" The room wheeled about him as he recognized the nightmare driver of the hornet car that had chased them from the airport.

SEVEN

"ARE YOU SURE?" STONER TURNED the book in his hands. The pages were bound with golden cord in its original knots. Nothing could have been added or subtracted from the original manuscript.

George's face flushed angrily. "Of course I'm sure." His fingertip stabbed at the page. "Do you think I'd draw something like that to scare Mindy?"

Stoner looked somberly at the page in question. There was no doubt in his mind that George had his dark side, they all did, but he doubted that George would show it.

George mistook his silent thoughts. "Oh, right. Humor me."

"No. You just hold on." Stoner flipped through a few more pages and then found another with weevils on it. This one was even darker and more terrifying than the previous, as it showed them pulling down a deer while the unicorn tried helplessly to defend it.

Leigh said, "The Johannsens," and sucked in her breath.

He shut the book abruptly. "We'll see about this in the morning." Stoner returned the book to the closet, turned off the light, heard Mindy's gasp, thought better of it, and turned the light back on.

Leigh and Mindy stared at him, two owl children with wide, frightened eyes. He paused, knowing he had to do better than that for them to go back to sleep. "Just a minute."

After a few minutes rummaging about in the den, he returned with a large, dark bound book in his hands. He placed it under the unicorn book.

"What's that?" Leigh whispered.

"The family Bible."

Relief passed through her face as she sagged back onto her pillows. Mindy nodded. "That oughta do it," she said with authority as he shut the closet door.

George glared at him as he ushered the boy out of the bedroom, leaving the girls to sleep.

The boy, only a few inches shorter than himself, balked in the hallway. "I never drew those pictures," he insisted in a hoarse whisper.

"We'll take care of it in the morning," Stoner returned. He watched George stalk away, resentment in the way he carried his shoulders. With a sigh, Stoner realized his pipe had gone cold.

Wolf, curled by the banister, raised his head and watched him. "Stay," Stoner said. He watched in satisfaction as the dog obeyed. He closed his eyes, thinking of Carrie. She had sent the kids to him, hoping they'd bond, just in case. "Jesus, lady," he murmured. "How you pull at my guts." Then he returned to sleep away what little night he had left.

Mindy lay quietly in bed. What Stoner had done to the book seemed to work, she thought with satisfaction. Like Dracula and garlic. She wished she'd thought of it sooner. Every day there had been more weevil pages no matter how fiercely she'd guarded it.

But George in her dream bothered her. He didn't seem to have heard what she'd heard. The weevil king wanted their mother. He wanted their mother worse than anything in the world and when they'd shown up, not bringing her, he'd been mad enough to eat them.

Mindy shivered. Her mother had to be warned. Even in the hospital, where there were white-gowned nurses and beige walls and lights on all the time, her mother had to know. Weevils weren't too smart, but pretty soon they were going to figure out that the children had left their mom back in New York, and the weevils would start to look for her there.

Mindy slipped out of the bed. The floor was chilly under her bare feet. It creaked slightly. She looked at Leigh, and then the closet, holding her breath. Nothing happened. Reassured, Mindy continued her journey out of the bedroom toward the downstairs phone.

Wolf woke up and came with her, padding down the staircase, his warm furry body pressed against hers. He even lay against her as she picked up the phone and hesitantly punched out the numbers she'd learned so painstakingly.

As the phone rang, she waited for the wheeze of the battered answering machine. Mom was in the hospital now, fighting the cancer, but she could leave a message on the old machine. Mom knew how to call up the old machine and make it sound off all the messages. She'd know Mindy had called her. Mindy thought warmly that maybe the hospital would let her return the call even if it was long distance. The ring of the phone rattled in her ear a second time.

"Hello?"

Mindy nearly dropped the phone at the static and sleep-blurred voice. Her mother wasn't supposed to be there! Then she clutched the receiver tightly.

"Hello? Who is this?"

Hot tears flooded her eyes as she said, "Mommy? Is that you?"

"Mindy, honey? What is it, baby? What's wrong?"

The voice sounded furry and weak, but Mindy knew it was her mother. She caught the sob in her throat. Why wasn't she at the hospital? Why wasn't she where she would be safe?

It stabbed her in one brief, hurting moment, that her mother had lied to her. She wasn't in the hospital at all. She just hadn't wanted Mindy to be around.

She squeezed the receiver. "Mommy, be careful. Watch out for weevils!" The sobs shut her throat. She gasped, unable to say anything else.

"Mindy, it's all right. Are you scared?" Then her mother coughed slightly, and then retched weakly.

Mindy had heard the sounds before. The medicine the doctors gave her at the hospital did that to her.

They ought never to have left her alone! "Watch out for weevils! I'm coming," Mindy hurled out, then crashed the phone down. It bounced out of the cradle, but she didn't notice it as she pushed Wolf away and ran back upstairs.

She dressed in the closet, then saw Leigh's old book pack hanging on a hook. Inside was a ten-dollar bill tucked away. Mindy hesitated, then jumped and brought the pack down. She shoved Rosebud and the Bible into it and left, going back down the stairs as quietly as she knew how. It was going to be a long walk back to New York.

EIGHT

CAROLINE WALSH STARED AT THE ceiling. Nausea rolled over her relentlessly as the phone line went dead. She felt guilt flood her, too. She should never have sent Mindy away, knowing how upset she was at having to go. The three of them, George and Leigh and she, had lied to Mindy about her having to stay at the hospital all the time. She hadn't wanted to lie, but the weekly therapy had been making her so ill, it was all she could do to drag herself around for the first few days. Then she had to endure four or five days, and go back, and start the cycle all over again.

The woman clenched her jaw, picked up the phone, and dialed Dave's number. The line buzzed at her. She waited a few minutes, then dialed again. Still busy. She'd call again in the morning and hope the line had cleared. And she would have to explain her lies to Mindy as gently as possible.

As she lay in the darkness, she thought of Dave Stoner and herself, and her deceased husband, Chris Walsh and herself, and sighed. Mindy had her weevils. She had her memories. She closed her eyes to uneasy sleep.

Stoner got up in the early gray edges of the dawn, showered, and dressed as quietly as he could. He let the kids sleep in, after their harrowing night. From work, he would call that family counselor Carrie had talked about. And when he had some answers, he would come back home and exorcise that book of Mindy's and the weird dreams they'd all had.

He noticed Wolf was asleep back in the kitchen. The phone had gotten knocked off its hook and he replaced it. Then he shrugged into his wool jacket and left.

Leigh bumped into George in the hallway and he scowled at her when she hushed his protest. "Mindy's still asleep," she added.

"Well, Stoner's gone already. He bolted out of here quick enough this morning and left us with that book."

That book, Leigh thought. *His own book has become the enemy*. She shuddered. "He said he'd take care of it."

"It or us," George said, not wanting an answer. He started to shoulder past her into the loft bedroom.

Leigh wrinkled her nose at the smell then and tweaked a piece of straw off his shirt. "Where have you been?"

"Mucking out the barn, it's called. I decided to let the two of you sleep in. Mindy gets too cranky when she's tired." He nudged the door open with a stockinged foot. He followed Leigh's glance downwards. "I had to leave my sneakers at the back door, all right? I mean, when you're cleaning out dirty straw, sometimes you step in the stuff, okay?"

Even if it hadn't been okay, Leigh doubted she would have had the nerve to say so. George straightened up and pushed his way into her bedroom, headed for the clump of blankets that was Mindy. For a cold instant, he thought his heart stopped. There was no movement from the bed. *Could a five-year-old die in her sleep?* ran through his mind. He shook it off angrily as he reached for the bed.

The still and empty hollow in the bed stared back at the two of them.

"Great." Then he turned on Leigh. "How could you not know if she was with you or not?"

There were purple shadows under Leigh's eyes. She blinked. "I don't know! I was just so tired. I slept like a log once everything settled down. And this morning, I didn't want to wake her."

George was ignoring her already. He got down on his hands and knees. "Where's her shoes?"

"What do you want her shoes for?"

He craned his head to look up at her, impatience written all over his face. For a moment, Leigh saw the shadow of her father in him, the shadow of him that she didn't like to remember. He'd never been a very patient man. "If her shoes are gone, stupid, then so is she."

"Gone where?"

"How should I know?"

The two children stared at each other.

"We're surrounded by woods," George said slowly.

"And if the weevils are in those woods—" Leigh snatched open the closet door. "Her shoes are gone! And my backpack! My ten dollars was in there!"

And, equally obvious, the Rosebud book and the Bible were gone, too.

George looked at Leigh. "She's not gone into the woods."

Leigh returned her brother's level stare. Defensively, he brushed his unruly shock of light brown hair from his eyes. She gathered her nerve. "She wanted Mom. She took my money. She's gone home!"

The two turned on their heels and raced downstairs.

"We've got to find her before Stoner comes back," George said as he leapt down the last three stairs. Wolf, in response to the commotion, came skidding out of the kitchen, a doggish grin splitting his black-and-silver mask. He jumped with them and barked happily.

George blocked the door to keep the dog from getting out. He let Leigh slide by, then slipped out himself, shutting the door on Wolf's puzzled woofs. He paused, his fingertips to the pane of glass on the kitchen door, and saw Wolf's head bob up and down, pulling at the curtain. "I hope I don't regret this," he muttered to himself before turning away and putting on his shoes.

The morning, though a bright blue sky, was still a little chill, and he could feel a mugginess in it. The humidity he was used to. He wondered if a brief thunder shower might be on its way. Leigh paused at the road.

"Which way do you think she went?"

"The way we came in. I don't think she'd go back in the woods." George sucked his lip, thinking of the black-and-red car and its menacing driver. "Let's hope she stuck to the road—and didn't let anyone pick her up." He broke into an slow jog.

Leigh panted to catch up with him. "I'm not going to run all the way to town," she protested.

He halted. "Look. She's five years old. Most of this country is farms or wilderness. And if there's wild dogs or weevils or whatever out here, they might find her before we do. She's walking—if we run, we just might have a chance!" He ran down the road, without waiting to see if Leigh would keep pace with him or not.

It was hot and sticky and dusty, and Leigh's backpack slid around on her shoulders. Mindy phuffed her bangs from her forehead. The road, rough at best, grabbed at the rubber toe of her sneaker again. She'd torn loose part of it, the strip that ran all the way around the shoe, whatever it was called—Mom was always repairing her sneakers with shoe goo—and it flapped with every step she took. She looked longingly at the trees and shrubs lining the road. She had forgotten to go to the bathroom before she'd left Mr. Stoner's and now the urge wouldn't go away. But she was too afraid to go pee in the bushes. If George had been here to stand guard—

Mindy stuck her lip out. She wouldn't think about it. She was going home where she belonged, even if it took her a year to walk there. Only she had hopes that ten dollars would buy her a bus ticket all the way back. Ten dollars was a lot of money. She might even have enough left over to buy a hamburger and a milk shake. Her mouth watered at the thought.

A branch crackled in the forest. Mindy looked askance and trotted a little faster down the road. A postman in a little white jeep had passed her, but other than that, she was all alone out here.

Except for whatever it was in the woods that moved along with her.

Mindy didn't know when she'd become aware that something else was out there. She'd been frightened at first, but the summer sun shone down and the road was hot enough. She knew if it was a weevil, it would stay in the shade. Enough sun could destroy a weevil, she was sure of it. But she thought it might be something else, for she sensed a curiosity from it, instead of an evil hunger, and she forgot all about it except when she thought of going into the bushes to pee. Then she would remember and hesitate and decide that it would be better to stay on the road.

At her back came the whine of a car. It screeched at the bend in the road and she moved over, listening to it race closer. He was driving awfully fast, she decided, and she moved off the road completely, just as the angry machine whooshed past in a sleek red-and-black blur. Mindy didn't even get a chance to see the driver hunched over the wheel.

She thought the car looked like a racing car and shrugged into the heavy backpack and stepped back onto the macadam.

The noise had just faded when a terrible squeal of brakes came. Then silence, then another squeal of rubber, and the whine began again, and Mindy's heart jumped as she realized the car was headed back toward her. Her pulse drummed. Cars and strangers. She'd heard all about cars and strangers from her nursery school and Mom. Mindy bolted from the road into the woods.

The branches slapped and tweaked at her, but she didn't

care. Her ears roared and she thought of her dreams, but she couldn't remember the beginning of it, how she'd gotten into the woods looking for her book, only that she was there. This wasn't like the dream at all, she decided, and plunged to a halt.

The car burned to a stop. Mindy went to her knees and, peering through the leafy brances swaying around her, watched the car. A door opened and a man got out—but there was something wrong about the way he stood and walked.

Mindy held her breath. Then the being turned toward her and took his sunglasses off, and she gasped.

Sharp muzzled and tuft eared, with eyes that smoldered crimson even in the sunlight. A weevil!

She put her hand to her mouth to keep from screaming.

He didn't look the same, quite. He wore a three-piece business suit, but it bent in all the wrong places, as though he wasn't used to standing up straight. His hat, like the kind Indiana Jones wore, hid most of his shaggy dark hair, and when he put the sunglasses back on, he looked almost human. *Almost.*

And he was definitely smarter than she thought a weevil could be.

Mindy's nerve broke. She pitched face forward into the bushes, running back down the way she had come, twigs cracking loudly under her desperate steps. She scampered as fast as she could, then tripped over something. Her breath stuck in her throat as she saw the outflung white leg and followed it to the half-eaten carcass of an old white horse. Black blood made the grass all twisted and dry. Flies and gnats buzzed up from a filmed-over eye clouded with death and fright. Shreds of flesh and intestines hung out onto the ground. She gagged, got to her feet, and began running again.

George staggered to a halt. He heard the car at their backs and said, "Let's see if we can flag him down. He might give us a ride." But when Leigh nodded wearily and George turned to raise his arms, he frowned. Then he grabbed her arm and dragged her flying off the shoulder into the shrubs.

Her temper broke. "What the hell was that for?" she snapped. Her hair was coming out of its braid and the ends stuck out all over.

But George stared at the road in icy fascination as the car screamed past them, none the wiser. *What was he after?* George wondered, and then knew. *Mindy.* "You're not going to believe this," he started, and proceeded to tell her about the crimson-eyed driver he'd seen following them Friday night from the airport.

Leigh looked at him critically. "You're kidding."

"No."

"Aliens from outer space."

"Or weevils. Or maybe just some guy that likes to wear contact lenses that scare the crap out of people." George got out of his crouch. "We've got to hurry."

Caution thrown to the wind, they took the middle of the road and ran, painfully at first, for both had stiffened up, then loosening into a stride. Leigh kept up with George's long legs, though her mouth opened and she breathed fitfully through it to do so.

The car screeched around a bend, nearly losing it, or so it sounded to George. He said to Leigh, "He's really moving."

She nodded wordlessly. Then the car sounds moved out of earshot, then a wild squeal of brakes. Her heart leapt into her throat and stayed there, a dry lump.

"Oh, God! He's got Mindy!" she gasped.

George pulled away from her, his long legs pounding, eating up the surface of the road. Gratefully, Leigh watched him go and staggered to a momentary halt before taking a burning breath and going after him.

Around the road's bend, she could hear the car revving up again and knew it was headed back toward them. George raced up the center line, all alone. No Mindy. Was it them the car was after?

George evidently had similar thoughts. He pivoted and

headed back to her, and for a second time they crouched in the bushes, but the car stopped out of their line of sight.

"Damn." George swatted a bug from the back of his neck. He lay down on his stomach, inching his way toward the shoulder. "What's he looking for?"

"What's he doing?"

"He just pulled over and stopped, on that curve up ahead. I can barely see him from here. But he's looking for something."

"Is it a . . . a weevil?"

"He looks like a businessman." George scratched. "But he's, like, all wrong. Like he has two elbows instead of one."

"Can you see his eyes?"

"Not from here." George was happy about that. He got up and began to work his way through the woods.

"What are you doing?"

"I want to know what he's looking for. Keep quiet, if you can."

Disgustedly, Leigh followed her brother, unhappy about his plan, but knowing he would leave her behind if he felt like it, and she was unhappier about that prospect.

They had gone about ten yards when all hell broke out ahead of them. Branches whipped and snapped as something came crashing at them. George let out a yelp and tackled it, and the two figures rolled around in the dirt and scrub grasses and needles.

Leigh stood up. "*George!* It's Mindy!"

The thrashing stopped abruptly and Mindy began to sob and she hugged George so tightly that he could hardly breathe. "It's dead! It's dead! Back there! D-D-Daisy's dead. The weevils killed her."

He stood up, holding her still, his face pinched and white. He looked at Leigh in utter panic. "Now we know for sure he was looking for Mindy."

"And with all this noise—"

"How far can you run?"

"All the way to Stoner's," Leigh answered, "if that thing is following us!"

The three of them bolted.

Behind them, the undergrowth swayed, and a snarling filled the air. Leigh looked over her shoulder to see the businessman giving chase—and to her horrified glance, he shed clothes as he did so, revealing a hairy body. He stopped, kicked off shoes, and sped after them. His eyes burned like red-hot embers. He dropped to all fours.

She plunged after George, screaming, "Run!"

The woods gave way to a sun-dappled clearing. George vaulted a bush and Leigh put her head down and followed, spurred by the beast at her heels. Its rasping growl broke off, as the beast swerved away.

The sunlight?

Leigh threw her head back, dazzled, and ran into a wall of flesh. She dropped in her tracks as the white mare threw up her head and squealed defiantly. She lay between the horse's hooves and panted for breath as George went to his knees, still hugging Mindy, his face a brilliant pink. The three children locked eyes.

The white mare reared and Leigh rolled out of the way, colliding against her siblings. The sunlight rayed down sharply and to Mindy's dazzled eyes, speared off the forehead of the mare. The weevil paused at the meadow's edge. It gnashed its teeth and stood back up.

The white mare pawed the grasses. She lowered her head menacingly, and the ray of sunlight pointed at the weevil.

"It's Rosebud!" Mindy burst out and began to cry.

NINE

THE WEEVIL PAUSED IN THE SHADE. He'd left the gray flannel pants of his business suit on, but they fit peculiarly, angled at the hocks of his legs. His odor was rank and damp, and musty as an old attic. The being grinned.

"Give them to me," he rasped.

The white mare tossed her head. "Never," she answered. In surprise, George heard her voice and thought of the rich contralto of an opera singer. It had class and depth . . . and strength.

He loosened his death grip around Mindy and got to his feet.

The mare shifted. She looked briefly at him. "Stay behind me," she warned. "Until we're both out of phase, he's deadly."

The weevil laughed hoarsely. It blurred, and then there were two. Another blur, and four stood at the meadow's edge, flinching at the sunlight, but daring them yet. Hot eyes burned into them.

Rosebud snorted, a definitely horsy sound. "Not a wise move, my enemy," she taunted him. "Shadow divided is never stronger." With a sudden lunge, she attacked the nearest, her sun-lance horn piercing the dark, hairy form. With a yelp and a snarl, it flared up and disappeared in a whiff of evil-smelling smoke.

Black smoke rings curled about Rosebud as she danced back into her place defending the children. Leigh stood carefully, but Mindy stayed crouched on the ground between them, her face shining with the glory of Rosebud's appearance.

Leigh reached out a trembling hand and touched the white mare's flank. She drew back as though burned. "But—yesterday—it *was* you—I put my hand through you—"

"Drawn here, out of phase, I was lost to you as quickly as I came. But today . . ." The full white mane flowed across her bowed neck with a life of its own. Leigh's hand ached to be wrapped in that mane and her legs to be astride the mare, part of her.

"What are you talking about?" George asked sharply.

He got no answer, for the three remaining weevils launched themselves at once, straight at them. With a snarl and a bound, they leapt.

Rosebud pivoted and kicked at the nearest two, but one got past, and George found himself with a foul, greasy handful that bore him to the ground, as it clawed for screaming Mindy.

He'd never liked wrestling in high school. But he dredged up his memories of the coach yelling hints at him, and threw his legs about the weevil, too. The creature rolled over and over with him, as George fought to pin the flailing arms. It snapped in his face with a breath that scorched, and the red eyes blazed. Fear shot through George then. He remembered the creatures that had been killed, torn limb from limb.

This beast had done that.

The wiry limbs contorted under him. George ducked his face as the weevil broke an arm loose, slashing at him. The weevil bucked suddenly and threw him to one side, then pounced for Mindy. George hit the ground hard, losing his breath.

"Leigh!" he gasped, even as the weevil caught Mindy by her ankle as she tried to scramble away. It began dragging her close.

His sister rushed in, kicking. "Leave her alone!" Her voice went higher and higher as she tried to stomp the weevil but it ignored her in its single-minded quest to get Mindy.

Rosebud stopped it with a single touch. Mindy screamed as the being flared into nothingness.

The white mare lowered her muzzle to the little girl. She whuffed gently across her face, erasing the marks of fear there. "You'll be all right for now," she said.

George got to his feet. He trembled. His biceps ached and cramped. If the shadow divided was weaker, he'd hate to meet a full-fledged weevil. Leigh dropped to her knees beside her sister.

George dusted off his hands. "When will they be back?" he asked.

"Tomorrow. Possibly tonight. The phases of the Twilight Gate are unpredictable. I only know by the pull . . . like the ebb and flow of some great ocean," the mare said abstractly.

George had the peculiar feeling that the language she spoke wasn't English, though he knew all the words. He couldn't quite grasp the sense of them. He brushed his hair back, trying to get it out of his eyes. "How are you . . . are you real?"

"As real as that gash across your knuckles," the mare said. She lipped at him, and the skin cleared, leaving him with a thin, pink line.

He stared at it, the breath suddenly tight in his chest. She could heal! "What . . ." he began, and his voice trailed away.

Mindy bolted to her feet. She shoved a fist deep into the pockets of her vest and came up with an unwrapped peppermint, its edges glommed with blue fuzz. She held it out and the mare took it delicately and crunched it. The little girl's face positively glowed. "Just like Mom wrote. Rosebud likes candy. I've been saving it for her for months, since . . . since . . ." Memory failed her and she frowned, trying to remember.

"Since we had dinner at the pizza place," Leigh prompted. She had been pulling on her honey blond hair, her eyes deep with thought. "You're an Indian spirit from another plane," she announced.

The white mare lifted her head. When she whuffed, it was with a peppermint aroma. "You might say that. Be that as it may, this is not my place or time, and the Gate across the pathways opens and closes . . . and I have been drawn, against my will, down a pathway that leads here and . . ." The white mare shuddered. "To even darker places, and to an in-between that I cannot leave. The weevils travel down those paths as well."

"You mean . . . they come from someplace else, too. Like another reality?" George caught on now, following Leigh's remarks. Alternate worlds, where magic existed instead of science. Or where another George had a father, because his father had made a different choice, once.

The creature looked at them. She had great violet eyes, deep and still as an undiscovered lake. "Be that as it may . . . the Gate measures a balance . . . an ebb and flow of light and dark . . . and things here are dangerously wrong. The weevils are an evil of their own, and don't belong here. Or am I wrong? Is this land of yours free of darkness?"

Leigh shook her head violently. "No."

"Ah." The white mare made a sad noise. "Then we must fight them." The light began to shine through her, and as Leigh put out a hand, she found the substance of the mare changing.

"The Gate is pulling me back," Rosebud said. She reared then, out of Leigh's reach. "I will be back—but beware, for when I am, the weevils will also, until we find the key to the Twilight Gate!"

With that, the mare blazed out of their sight, as the three children stared, entranced.

"I saw the horn, didn't you?" Mindy said with joy as she looked from brother to sister.

George muttered, "No," but no one heard him.

Out of their sight, a red-and-black car wavered on the road. Its driver straightened. He grimaced, a gesture showing his fangs, replaced his fedora on his head, and his sunglasses on his face, and got in, just before the car disappeared.

The walk home seemed interminable. Even though the weevils had supposedly left with the white mare, George found himself looking back over his shoulder. The asphalt grew hot enough to burn through the soles of his sneakers, which were thin, anyway. The blue sky paled and then grew dappled with clouds. Mindy walked slower and slower, until he finally took her up and tried to carry her. First he tried to carry her sitting on his shoulders until his neck cramped and he thought his skull was going to drop off.

Then he shifted to carrying her in his arms. But his arms, already stiff and cramped from his wrestling match, refused to take the strain. Finally, he ended up taking her piggyback, and though he staggered hunched over, it was a better arrangement than the others.

Leigh trotted along beside him. Her face was flushed pink with excitement, or maybe it was sunburn. "Wasn't she beautiful?" she said for the millionth time.

"Who?" George asked, as though he didn't know.

"Rosebud! The unicorn!"

He stopped on the burning roadway. "I didn't see any unicorn. Or a white mare, either."

"You what?" Her mouth opened in astonishment. She looked just like Mom did when he'd done something really awful, like toilet-papered the boys' locker room. Except that Mom didn't get all pink. She usually went white.

"No," he said carefully. "I think I saw the old mare, that dairy mare, and she frightened off a couple of really scroungy-looking dogs. Wild dogs, I'd guess."

"But George—!" Then his sister pressed her lips tightly together. "Nobody would believe us, right?"

"Right."

"Uh-huh," asserted Mindy sleepily from George's back. "Rosebud is supposed to be a secret."

"Yeah, well . . . your running away had better be a secret, too," he said.

"Wasn't running away." Her chin gouged his shoulder. "Was going home."

Leigh patted her shoulder. "I know," she said softly.

George hiked his sleepy bundle up a little and started walking again. "Why?"

"I called Mom on the phone, to leave a message about the weevils." Mindy paused. "You guys lied! You sent me away! What if—what if—she dies before we get to go home again?"

George and Leigh looked at one another. Privately, they'd both thought that, but had been too afraid to admit they'd thought it.

"She won't die," Leigh said firmly.

"She might."

"The chemotherapy has an eighty percent chance of curing her completely."

"What's that mean?" Mindy asked.

George shrugged. He answered, "It means, eight times out of ten, it works."

Mindy had a native instinct for numbers. She countered, "What about the other two times?"

They walked in silence a long time before Mindy realized she'd made her point, and said, "See!" Then she said,

"But the weevils are more dangerouser. They want me—and her. I don't know why."

Leigh put a sweat-soaked strand of hair behind her ear. "What is the Twilight Gate?"

"It's the way they get in and out." George took a deep breath and stopped again. Mindy was getting really heavy. "It could be anything. Like a rip in the fabric of time, or maybe a warp through space."

"Or a book?" Leigh asked softly.

He lowered Mindy to the road. "Maybe."

The three of them stared at each other. Then Leigh said, "But how could you do something like that?"

"I don't know." George shifted uneasily. "Maybe my mind is what's warped."

"Or maybe, just maybe," Leigh said softly, reaching forward and grabbing her brother's hand and showing him the newly healed scar, "Rosebud is supposed to be right where she is!"

TEN

BACK AT THE HOUSE, MINDY ATE canned chicken noodle soup, peanut butter crackers, drank three glasses of ice water, and went upstairs to go to sleep.

She completely missed the undercurrent of excitement flashing between George and Leigh, and they contained it until she left.

Leigh took a sponge and swept up the cracker mess from the kitchen table. Wolf eagerly finished off the last of it from her hand as she held it down to him. He tried to lick the sponge, too, but she rinsed it off and put it away. George sat thoughtfully at the table.

"Mindy tried to tell us," he said.

Leigh's chair scraped noisily against the floor as she pulled it out. "Who would have believed it? Where would we get a unicorn from, anyway?"

"Maybe we dreamed it." He rubbed the back of his hand thoughtfully. "But I've never had a dream that left scars before."

"And even if we did dream it—who's to say that's not another kind of world. Maybe it does exist." She waited for George to make Twilight Zone sounds to mock her, but he didn't. He just took a big gulp of ice water.

"Then how do we reach it?"

"We try the book first." George pulled Leigh's backpack toward him. He hesitated before opening the flap. "We already know about the weevil pictures. I suggest we look at it, page by page, and see if we can come up with something."

"And if we can?"

"Then we pull Rosebud into our world, and go get Mom and introduce them. And then we let a spirit mare do what it does best."

"And she'll be cured."

"Yeah."

Silence reigned in the kitchen a moment. It was broken by the ignominious sound of Wolf scratching at a flea. Then Leigh took a quivery breath and pulled the unicorn book out.

Page by page, it was a testament to her brother's talent—and his worry over their mother. Leigh ran her fingers over the pages, unable to bear the pain of what she saw when she really looked into them. It was as though their mother had been hurt, terribly hurt, and sought healing. Rosebud had been painted triumphantly as though to say, Good does exist! And here it is! Valiant and brave through all its suffering.

George said nothing as Leigh turned the pages, and she wondered what he thought. She tried to remember when he had started the book, but she could only come up with memories of his sketching late at night. She thought she recognized the woods beyond Stoner's house. She hadn't noticed that before. She bent over a page. She traced it with her fingertip.

"Look here."

George leaned close. Leigh outlined a tree in the background. She'd never noticed before, but etched into its trunk was a heart, and that heart outlined the initials *CP* and *DS*.

"Caroline Palmer and Dave Stoner," George said flatly. "I saw that tree out back. I sketched it in." George had a faraway look in his eyes as his face lifted. "He said she was always drawing unicorns, too."

"But she's never been here!"

"Maybe not. Maybe. She was married to him, before."

George pushed himself away from the table and stood up. "I'll show you."

Leigh loped after him. At the edge of the woods, he stopped and took his bearings. Then he headed to a stand of trees not far from the shed.

The carving had changed, in the nearly twenty years. The heart had elongated and stretched, and the initials pushed out, but in the black-and-white bark of the tree, Leigh couldn't deny what had been carved there. She caught her breath. "Do you think—do you think she was hurting even then?"

"They hated each other enough to get divorced, didn't they?" her brother answered as he turned his back on her and strode back to the house.

Leigh picked up the book again and tried to ignore George's abrupt outburst as they returned to the kitchen.

"There's a link to the spirit mare, between us and Mom, and Mom and here. If only we can figure out a way to use that." He rocked back in his chair as Leigh hurriedly flipped past one of the weevil pages.

"We'll find it somehow," Leigh said. She spread the book out, and they squeezed their chairs together, searching.

Stoner looked out from his vehicle. The lake was still shifting, changing pH, and he knew that soon it would go dead, too acid to support life. A shame. Spirit Lake had been a spiritual home for the Indians for generations and even now carried with it a kind of mystic serenity. It had been Carrie's favorite spot when they were first married before he'd been drafted. It was on a decline he could not stop, no matter what he tried. And, like his marriage, he couldn't remember when it had started.

With a sigh, he rubbed the back of his neck. Carrie's doctor in New York, Dr. Taslitz, was supposed to have called back hours ago at the job site but hadn't. He thought about the kids again, and worried, and decided to call it a day.

He'd already pretty much decided what he was going to do, anyway. Kids always had trouble accepting their parents as people, up until a certain stage. Those pages had been in the book, surely—a real book, with villains and troubles, besides pretty pictures—and George was obviously denying having drawn them. In his own way, he was having as much trouble accepting his mother's cancer as Mindy was.

He'd simply take the book away from them tonight, and talk to them. He'd have to see if he could bring their fears out into the open. He'd known it was going to be a difficult summer, though he hadn't quite anticipated this. George's surliness, here and then gone, was more down the line. He hadn't expected Leigh, though six years younger than Carrie when he'd first met her, to be a carbon copy of her. And Mindy—an arrow through his heart, the worst of any of the three. He'd talk to Inga tonight and see if she was willing to take on watching the three kids this summer. He'd decided not to leave them on their own where their fears could feed off each other.

The goats were bleating hungrily in the shed when he drove up, and the two older children, deaf to their charges, looking over the unicorn book on the kitchen table. Guiltily, they ran to feed the goats and let them out into the corral for exercise. Stoner watched them and decided to give the goats to the Johanssens for the summer, too.

He stood by the kitchen door. Wolf made a wide berth about the kitchen table. He pushed his wet black nose at the edge, growled at the book, then came and stood by Stoner, pushing his head up under the man's hand for a scratch.

"Don't you go getting spooked on me," Stoner said distractedly.

George loped back across the yard. The man and boy eyed each other. "How'd the day go?" asked Stoner.

George shrugged. The two of them both watched Leigh playing tag with the goats in their pen.

Stoner cleared his throat. "Where's Mindy?"

"Still asleep. We took her out on a hike this morning."

George gave a lopsided grin. "We wore her out more than we intended to."

"Fresh air. It'll do it every time. Is she . . . feeling better?"

The boy hesitated. Then he said, "She called Mom last night. She was really mad at us this morning."

"She knows Carrie is still living at the apartment?"

"Yeah."

This was something Stoner had anticipated, a normal problem. And it fit with having found the phone off the hook that morning. "I'll have a talk with her when she wakes up."

"No." George flushed slightly. "I mean, it's all right now. We talked with her. I think she understands now."

"All right." Stoner decided not to challenge George at the moment. All three of them were too upset. But soon, very soon, the boy was going to have to accept the fact that Stoner, not George, was the adult in charge here.

As Leigh came into the kitchen, George whispered, "Remember, it's ten miles from here."

She flashed him a worried look. "I can't walk ten miles!"

"No . . . but I can drive it."

"You couldn't!"

"I could. Mom let me practice a couple of times." He said nothing else, but looked pale.

Leigh shut her mouth on her protest as Stoner entered the kitchen then, a waking Mindy in his arms. She looked to the table.

"Where's the book?"

"Mindy and I just put it away," Stoner said.

George signaled Leigh to drop it, and so she did. She smiled a little. "Where it's safe?"

Mindy answered, her sable bangs puffing up and down on her forehead as she nodded emphatically.

"That's good," Leigh said. She turned away. She tried not to think of the ritual she and George had planned out, a ritual drawn from the book, to bring Rosebud firmly into this world. "How about dinner?"

"Sounds good," Stoner answered as he lowered Mindy into a chair. "What do you have in mind?"

"I can make chili dogs," she responded.

He winced. "How about we barbecue some hamburgers? With fruit salad and chips?"

George grinned. "That sounds better!" And the two men went off to do another, more familiar, ritual.

Late at night, waiting for George's soft knock, she and Mindy lay, listening to Dave Stoner wrestle with his nightmares on the other side of the wall.

Mindy whispered in her ear, "What's wrong with him?"

"Nightmares."

"Weevils?"

"No, I think maybe he dreams about the war he was in. Stuff like that." She hugged Mindy. The couch in the den creaked as Stoner got up, and she heard him pad his way softly down the hall to the bathroom. The medicine cabinet door squeaked as he opened it.

It was all going perfectly. George had seen the sleeping pills in the cabinet earlier. They had all crossed their fingers that the stress of the last few days would lead Stoner into taking them. She listened as he came back and lay down again, and in a little while, he was snoring gently.

As she got up, fully dressed, and urged Mindy to, the little girl said, "When we get Rosebud, we'll have her help Mr. Stoner, too."

Leigh answered, "Right," though she wondered if unicorns and Indian medicine mares could cure war, too.

The bedroom door across the way creaked open cautiously and George came out. "The keys are downstairs. Let's go."

Wolf gave them a curious look as they picked up the car keys, a flashlight, and the map George had hidden while doing the dishes. He settled down as George said, "Stay," and the three of them slipped out the back door.

Mindy sat excitedly in the front seat between them.

"Are you going to use the four-wheel drive?" Leigh asked.

"No."

"But the map shows some rough terrain once we take the side road."

"Right." His hands clutched the wheel tensely.

Mindy looked at them. "Are we gonna be like Big Foot?" she asked. "Are we gonna roll over rocks and everything?"

"No."

"Why not?"

"Because. I. Don't. Know. How," George said through clenched teeth.

Mindy decided not to pursue the thought further.

They nearly missed the gravel road, but finally found it, and though George crunched over a bush making the turn and Mindy slid off the seat and came to rest under the dashboard, everything went fine. It had to have been more than ten miles. It seemed to take forever.

When he stopped the car by the lakeshore and turned off the lights, and they all got out, Leigh's flashlight was a very feeble candle in the darkness. The sounds of nighttime crowded all around them. Water lapped faintly on rocks. It smelled bad, and there was an oppressive feeling about them, like a cloak.

They couldn't see far enough, except for the lake's surface, where the moon shone faintly down. It made a white pool of wavering reflection. Something plopped. An oily slick rippled toward them.

"Let's get started," George said briskly. He pulled Leigh's backpack, which they'd filled with things, out of the car.

Mindy started right to the lake and Leigh said sharply, "Don't go too close!"

"You're not Mom," the little one retorted, but she paused, anyway, at the sharp ledges of the lake. Rocks and broken saplings jutted upward. She had expected perhaps sand and twisty grasses leading gently down to the water's edge. But this was sharp and sudden.

George busily made a smallish circle of white candles. He looked up. "When I get ready to light these, I want both of you inside."

Mindy's dark hair blended into the darkness of the night as she looked dubiously to him. "Is this gonna work?"

He shrugged. "I don't know. I *think* so, but I don't know."

"Well, I do," said Leigh. "It's going to work."

"If we had the book . . ." Mindy's words trailed off.

"Well, we don't."

George pulled a long strip of white paper out of the backpack, and with it, a Scotch tape dispenser. He began to loop it. "All we've got is that page we tore out."

Mindy's lip quivered. "From my book."

"We agreed. This is all for Mom." Leigh stood up and eyed her.

The silence crept in all about them. It was almost as if the wilderness were listening to them, to their high, childish voices drifting across the lake. The lake was hurting, too, she could feel it. Leigh shivered and swatted at a mosquito on her arm.

George seemed oblivious to the mood. He reached out for Mindy and tugged her inside the circle of candles. "Hold this for me."

She did, at arm's length. "What's it called again?"

"A Möbius strip. It—well, never mind. It's just funny, kind of an infinite loop."

"What's in-fen-it mean?"

"Forever. It's a kind of forever loop."

"Oh." Mindy rubbed her big brown eyes thoughtfully.

Leigh said, "I'm ready." She held a piece of notepaper filled with her handwriting, the flashlight illuminating it for her to read.

"Right. Okay, here goes." George bent over and lit the candles quickly, burning his fingers once. The squat stumps burned hesitantly in the dampish night air, but caught, and their orange glow made the night a little warmer. "We three children of Caroline Walsh call you, Rosebud, the Unicorn. Hear us now." His voice dipped and strengthened, deepening suddenly.

"Give it," George said, and Leigh pressed a tiny, beribboned lock of blond hair into his hand. It was one of several she had pressed into her diary. She'd added feathers and beads to it.

Mindy watched. She shoved her own small hand into her vest pocket, where the torn-out page of her book resided. It crinkled comfortingly under her touch.

George took the lock of their mother's hair and traced it along the Möbius strip. Mindy watched, fascinated, as it changed pathways mysteriously along the loop. He traced its journey three times as Leigh chanted their summoning.

He finished as she did.

They both turned to Mindy, who pulled out the page. It fluttered in her hand, and the breeze came up a little, bending the candle flames around their feet. He dropped the curl of hair, so fine, so blond, into the middle of the page. He sketched a gate, quickly, like an opening out of a storm cloud, with a unicorn leaping through its shadowy interior. The picture took him long moments to do, but neither girl complained. His hands still shook from the drive. He hated driving. He crumbled the page into a hard ball and gave it back to Mindy. He nodded. Mindy took a deep breath and cocked her arm.

Together the three of them shouted, "We open the Gate! We charge you, Rosebud, with answering our call!"

Mindy had practiced all evening until dark and her shoulders ached as she threw back her head and watched the wad of paper sailing through the night. It seemed to have wings of its own, and all three children aaahed softly.

The arc rose until it crossed the moonbeam rays shining down on the lake, and then it fell, splashing into a puddle of reflection. The water sprinkled upward, then churned and foamed. It spurted upward as though driven, beads of crystal shining.

Mindy hopped. "It's Rosebud!"

"No . . . that's the reflection," Leigh started to correct her, and drew her back before she could break the circle of candlelight, and her objection staggered to a halt in her throat.

Something did boil in the lake. Something pure and white was being born in the fountain of water. George grabbed her arm, hard, and she said "Ow" so faintly no one else heard her.

The spray of water continued, and a thrashing filled the air as the white beast swam vigorously toward them, toward the shore, and there was no doubt in any of their minds that they watched an element, a spirit, being born.

She sprang upward, over the rocks and pointed saplings, leaping out of the water, and shook herself, spraying drops everywhere. Half the candles sputtered out, but George felt the warmth of her presence.

He reached toward her, but the mare tossed her head upward, moonlight glancing off like a spiraled horn to pierce the night.

"What have you done?" she cried in that full, rich voice of hers. "The Gate opened but a moment . . . I was going home, finally . . . when you pulled me back and now—now the Gate is closed to me, forever."

"Mommy needs you," Mindy cried and leapt across the candle stubs to throw her arms around the bowed neck of the mare.

Rosebud quivered. "No," she said softly. "You don't understand. Before, the weevils came because I was here . . . and a balance was needed. Now that I'm here and can no longer go back—their Gate is opened. They will flood your world. Oh, children! What have you done!"

ELEVEN

GEORGE'S WARM FEELING WENT icy. "What do you mean?"

The mare, who had dropped her muzzle to lip Mindy's shoulder affectionately, looked up. "Weevils . . . the Shadow-touched, if you will . . . are now free to flood your world. Will be as long as I am here. Now you will have living nightmares to face, along with whatever evil your world has already spawned."

"But our mother—"

Rosebud looked to Leigh. The mare blinked in the beam of the flashlight, and Leigh flicked it away. "Our mother needs you."

"Have the weevils hurt her? Is she Shadow-touched?" The mare's ears pricked forward eagerly and George thought, she's like a soldier, a soldier of good, and this is a war she fights.

"No—it's cancer and, ah—"

"What is this cancer?"

Leigh's hand trembled visibly. It made the flashlight beam bounce up and down in her hand. "It's a disease . . . a sickness. She has growths in her lungs. And, and . . ." Leigh's words stumbled to a halt as her voice broke.

The mare looked to George. Her nostrils flared. "Growths?"

"Tumors," Mindy blurted. "And they're killing her."

"Ahhhh." The white mare sighed. "An illness of your world. But not an injury."

"No."

"Then I cannot help you. My powers are universal against wounds, but the evils of this world, I'm afraid I have little chance against. This is something you must conquer yourselves. Have you no herbalists? Holistic healers?"

"What?"

"I think she means doctors," George said wearily. "She's been seeing them, and there's a good possibility they can help but—Mindy thought when we saw you—our legends say the unicorn can heal."

"Alas." The mare lowered her head and gave Mindy an apologetic whuff. "I'm so sorry, my children. Legends are not always what they seem." She jerked her head up suddenly, as a branch cracked like a shot through the night. "I cannot stay. Weevils will be coming as soon as their Gate opens, and this time, they will not be forced back as they were once. As long as it's dark, my presence is a mortal danger for you."

George was aware that the night hung heavy over them, moist and warm, and even as he looked up, a low rumbling issued.

Leigh shivered. "It's going to rain."

"We'd better go."

Mindy threw an arm about the retreating white mare's neck. "No! We can't leave her. Now she's as helpless as Mom!"

The two older children looked at the misty white beast. "Can you follow us?" George asked slowly.

"I dare not. I will endanger you."

"Then where—"

Rosebud answered gently, "I will stay about in these woods, as I have off and on since I was first drawn from my world."

"Will you . . ." George cleared his throat, feeling the ache of having done something terribly wrong for the right reasons, and now being unable to undo it. "Will you be all right?"

"For a time. There is an illness in this land that wearies me." She looked back at Spirit Lake. "Therein lies my Gate . . . decayed and as diseased as this world . . . though once I might still have been able to return. Perhaps—" She looked toward the children. "Perhaps it's up to you to heal me." With that, abruptly, she threw her head up and neighed, a defiant trumpeting that blended with the lightning that flashed across the summer sky. "They come! Run, children! Run! And beware the Shadow-touched!"

She leapt away, dragging Mindy's hands from around her neck as an eerie howl broke. George jumped for Mindy, grabbed her up, and threw her in the backseat of Stoner's car. Hot raindrops began to splatter them. Leigh stood rooted in place, her knees locked.

She twisted and looked over the far end of the lake. Burning coals of eyes raced toward them.

"Leigh!" George screamed.

Her knees buckled then. She grabbed her backpack and sprinted to the far side of the car, rain blurring her eyes.

"Roll up the windows and lock the doors!" George commanded as he turned the key in the starter.

The engine rolled over, sputtered, and died.

Thunder obliterated his curse. He pumped the accelerator and Leigh said, "Don't do that— you're flooding it!"

"What do you know?"

"That's what Daddy always used to say."

Mindy's voice quavered from the backseat. "Here they come."

Leigh looked to her right. She could smell their hot, sulfurous breath, even as they snarled and bounded across the last ten feet of clearing. Dark, furry bodies of hatred and evil. Shadow-touched, she thought wildly, even as Mindy let out a piercing scream.

The car jerked into movement. Dirt and gravel spun out from its tires and they shot away into the darkness.

There was a thump on the back window. Leigh turned, grabbed Mindy, and began to haul her onto the front seat. The car slewed around a bend and the weevil was thrown off. Slaver from his drooling jaws left a wet trail behind him on the rear window, but the pounding rain washed it off. Leigh and Mindy hugged each other tightly.

George drove with more speed and confidence on the way back and it seemed their hearts had barely slowed their wild beating before he turned into the gravel driveway. He turned off the headlights and motor and put it into neutral. As he started to swing out, Leigh hissed, "What are you doing?"

"Pushing the car in. I don't want to wake up Stoner."

"I'll help. Mindy, you steer."

The two of them pushed the heavy vehicle up the driveway, their sneakers crunching on the wet gravel. The rain had stopped, momentarily, leaving the air fragrant with its moisture.

As the car rolled into place, Leigh sighed and straightened. She looked to George's lanky height.

"No one is safe now," she said.

"I guess not. Not until we find a way to send her back." He straightened too. Silently they walked around to the car doors. George reached in for Mindy as Leigh leaned past to get her backpack.

Behind them, an angry voice grated. "What the hell is going on here?"

George woke to a muffled knock on his bedroom door. He straightened out his twisted sheets and blankets as Leigh slipped in quietly. From the graying at the window, he could tell it was nearly dawn.

"What is it?"

She sat silently at the bed's edge. "He was sure mad, wasn't he?"

"Yeah."

She wove her fingers in and out, opened her hands up, then rewove her fingers. "How much do you think we can tell him?"

"Not much. And . . . I don't know . . . this stuff goes way back," George said. "Way back to when Mom and him first dated. Maybe he's . . . Shadow-touched, too."

"The nightmares."

George nodded solemnly.

"Maybe that's why Mom left him."

"Maybe."

Leigh took a shuddering breath. "Then we're in this all alone."

"Yeah. But we knew that from the first, right? Just us and Mom against the world."

She put her face in her hands. "I'm scared."

"Me, too." George awkwardly patted her shoulder, thinking that it was bad enough to be scared about Mom's dying, and now this. All of them could be caught by the weevils. A sharpness caught at him. He didn't want to die. His throat closed up.

Leigh let out a muffled groan.

"Go back to bed," he said. "I'll think of something."

Morning in the city. Caroline clutched a sweater about her shoulders, even though the day promised heat and smog and humidity. Cabs were nowhere, and she'd just missed the bus in a choking cloud of exhaust. Her shopping bag swung from her elbow. Cans of soup rattled against each other, pounding to death the head of lettuce and fresh oranges she'd also just bought. She contemplated her arm as she pulled the sweater into place again. Slender as she'd ever been . . . no, thin. She smiled slightly, thinking *What a way to diet*, then gritted her teeth as a wave of nausea battered her insides.

And this morning, before going out, she'd lost two huge handfuls of hair. She'd quickly tied a scarf about her head. She'd known that would come. It was typical of chemotherapy, but it saddened her anyway. Was it worth losing all that she'd had, all that she'd become, just to fight this disease?

She hurried down the sidewalk, headed home, fighting a shiver. It would be a long walk, but another bus was due to come along and she didn't want to just stand at the stop and wait for it. If she kept in motion, she didn't have to think. And she was in a hurry. She wanted to call Dave and ask about Mindy. Her shoes clicked along the pavement, brown bag rustling in accompaniment.

Someone brushed past her, and she stopped, and heard an echoing step halt also. Caroline's heart jumped, and she looked around. She saw nothing in the late-morning shadows.

She'd lived all these years in the city and never been mugged.

She put her head down and hurried back into step. Did she look like a victim? Could anyone tell by looking at her that she couldn't fight back? Couldn't give chase? Dammit, could just barely *live?*

Other walkers thinned out. She stopped to look in a tailor's window. The glass was old and dirty and filmed over with grime, distorting her reflection. She heard another step pause. A hard step. New, unrelenting leather soles slapping against the pavement. Caroline took a deep breath and turned back up the street, looking desperately for a cab. Fear sucked at her lungs, taking away what little breath she had. She was being followed, she was certain of it.

She began to hurry. The street ahead was nearly deserted. The gray and brownstone buildings showed her aging and unfriendly faces. There was no one who could help her if she needed it.

Caroline looked over her shoulder. She saw a thin, wiry man in a gray business suit and overcoat, fedora, and sunglasses, keeping pace with her. Overcoat and sunglasses? He looked wrong. She let her sweater drop from her thin shoulders and stuffed it into her bag. The fresh lettuce would further suffocate and wilt, but she didn't care.

Caroline stopped for a light. There were two other people there, standoffish, watching the signal, waiting for a change, as if no one else in the world existed but them. She tried to calm her breathing and coughed instead, and one of the other waiters moved unconsciously away.

Someone moved up behind her. She looked back. It was the wiry man in the hat and coat. His sunglasses reflected back her stricken reflection. She thought to herself, *Do I look that scared?* then hurried away as the signal changed.

The man kept following.

Her purse slipped from her shoulder and tangled around her ankle, bringing her to an abrupt halt. Caroline bent nearly in two and tried to pull it up by the strap. Someone bumped into her from behind and grasped her arm sharply, just above the elbow. His breath was hot.

Caroline jerked her arm back before she even saw it was him. Her movement knocked his glasses askew slightly.

Two hot, red eyes glared at her. Caroline gasped. Her mouth fished for air in a silent scream. Her purse came swinging up from her ankles, narrowly missing the man's face. A bus pulled into the curb behind her.

Caroline twisted away and ran, as the doors hissed open. She dropped in her fare and then sagged onto a seat, and watched as the man on the street adjusted his sunglasses and hat and watched her fade into the traffic. He turned toward her and she wondered who he could have been, and how he did that sick trick with his eyes, and why he'd chosen her, of all people. And as she turned away from the street and clutched her groceries, she thought of Mindy's voice in the night, over the phone.

"Watch out for weevils!"

Caroline Walsh shuddered. She wiped a sudden fringe of perspiration from her forehead.

And, despite the sweat and heat of the crowded bus, felt icy cold.

TWELVE

STONER WOKE IN THE MORNING, his eyes grainy and swollen with lack of sleep. He brushed his teeth quickly to get rid of the furry taste of morning, then showered and shaved, and dressed quietly. Behind the bedroom doors, he heard the children snoring gently. They were dead to the world this morning, and no wonder, after all they'd gone through last night.

Dave paused in the hallway, turning his shirt collar down. Whatever had possessed George to take the car and try driving, he didn't know. He was fairly sure that they hadn't been trying to go home, though, but other than that, George's story about "just wanting to drive" was pretty lame. To put himself in George's shoes, the last thing he'd want to do would be to take along two witnesses like his sisters. No, they'd been up to something last night. The two older ones had nearly jumped out of their skins when he'd confronted them by the kitchen door. It was probably that damn book again. Maybe they'd gone out in the full of the moon to try and exorcise it or something.

Wolf met him at the bottom of the stairs. He pushed his wet nose into Dave's hand, seeking reassurance.

"What is it, boy, eh? Whole world turned upside down, huh." He scratched the dog's ear. Wolf seemed content to pad behind him into the kitchen, his nails ticking on the floor.

Stoner fixed a pot of coffee, filled his thermos, and left, no time for breakfast. The children would just have to learn to live with their traumas. After all, he had—hadn't he?

But as he drove to the job site, it struck him that if he had, he wouldn't be a fortysomething unmarried man. A man with nightmares so terrifying that he couldn't remember them when he bolted awake at night.

Stoner clenched his jaw and thought of calling Caroline.

It wouldn't be the easy thing for him to do. Even now, hearing her voice made it hard for him to breathe, remembering that, not once, but twice, he'd had her, and thrown her away again. There was the summer just out of high school when they'd been engaged, and then married, just before he'd been drafted. And then, there was the last summer, seven years ago, when George and Leigh had been at summer camp. Christopher Walsh had walked out on Caroline, but she'd sent the children away unknowing, and they'd run into each other accidentally in New York. He'd gone for an architectural conference, and she'd been delivering legal papers to a client at the hotel.

His jaw flexed as he thought of Christopher Walsh coming back to her and he'd let Caroline go without a fight a second time . . . let her go because of the selfsame children he was harboring now. The children plus Mindy. Not that the children would care one way or the other, because they'd had their father and their mother, and all had been right in their world.

Stoner looked up in surprise as his car swung into a driveway and he realized he'd been driving automatically, without seeing the road. It was a good thing the road had been clear. He got out of the car, deciding to slay one dragon at a time. First, the room addition. Then, the children.

They all slept in. With no adults to protest the caffeine, Leigh grabbed the coffeepot, claiming she needed it to wake up. Mindy busily stirred around the last bite of French toast in the buttery, syrupy soup on her plate, then stuffed it into her mouth. She looked rather like a chipmunk, Leigh thought, as she sipped her café au lait. It did send a bracing jolt through her body.

"We'll have to send her back." George announced his decision as he cleaned up Mindy's plate.

"That goes without saying," Leigh responded.

"Oh, it does? Well, how come nobody around here has said it yet."

"Because we don't know how. We don't even know how we got her here."

Mindy was licking off her sticky fingers and stopped, solemnly, her hand in front of her lips. "We got her through the picture."

"Oh, come on, Mindy. George's got a big enough head as it is," Leigh said scornfully.

"Maybe not." George dried the clean plates thoughtfully. "But every time I draw something anymore, something weird happens. Like I'm being haunted."

"Just like that."

"Why not?" George's eyes challenged her. He had that narrow, mean look to his face that he never had when they had both parents. Since Dad had died, he'd started arguing so much with her.

Leigh decided she didn't like that look. She set her coffee cup down. "Nothing is that simple. If it was, we'd have unicorns and cartoon characters popping up all over."

He blinked once. "Rosebud thinks she was drawn here first, and the bad guys came after. But what if it was the other way around. What if the bad guys came first, to haunt us, and she was pulled in to balance?"

"Why would anyone want to haunt you?"

"Because of . . . what I did."

"What did you do?"

His lips closed stubbornly and he didn't answer.

"That doesn't explain anything. And how would one of your drawings get them here?"

Mindy stopped blowing bubbles in her mug of milk and looked up, wearing a frothy white moustache. "It's like a house," she said. "There's only one front door."

The two older children looked at her. She shrugged and went back to blowing good-luck bubbles in her milk.

George pointed. "Or gate. I think she's got it. Earth is like a gigantic house, and there's only one front door."

"Then how do the weevils get in?"

"The back door? A crack in the window? Someplace that ought to be locked against them, but isn't."

"So," Leigh said softly. "All we need to do is open Rosebud's door, and the crack that the weevils slip through will be shut again."

"Something like that."

"Then we'll need the book."

Both of them looked at Mindy. She snorted into the milk, sending it fountaining. When they'd cleaned up the mess, she said, "Mr. Stoner and I hid it and I promised it would stay."

"But Mr. Stoner doesn't know about Rosebud, and he can't find out."

Mindy's eyebrows went up, nearly meeting the dark fringe of her bangs. "Because he's bad?"

"We don't know. He has all those nightmares and stuff. Maybe the weevils can get to grown-ups faster than they get to us. He took the book away, didn't he?"

"Careful, George," Leigh said.

He flashed an angry look at her. "Look, I'm going

about this the only way I know how. I don't want to draw anything new. We've got to get a handle on this."

"That doesn't make it right. Stoner hasn't done anything to us. He's been nice."

"Rosebud said beware of the Shadow-touched."

Leigh's next argument died on her lips. She couldn't counter that. She drained the last of her coffee from the mug. She wished she knew what to do. She wished she could talk to Mom. She looked at George. "What would Mom do?"

He froze. Then, stiffly, said, "I don't know."

The silence in the kitchen was broken by Wolf's eager yelp at the kitchen door. Startled, Leigh jumped in her chair.

"I didn't hear his car," George said as he bolted to the kitchen window and pushed the curtain aside.

The finely etched head of the spirit mare shone back at him and Mindy let out a squeal of joy.

"It's Rosebud."

They boiled out of the door and into the gravel yard where the white creature waited for them. She nodded at the barn. "You have duties awaiting you, I believe?"

The spirit mare waited for them while they fed the kids and let them out to pasture. Wolf circled her gleaming beauty cautiously, pausing once or twice to sniff at her feathered legs.

Rosebud stamped once, in warning, and he kept clear after that, though clearly puzzled in a doggish way as to what manner of creature it was that spoke. She swished her tail, bothered in no way by the barnyard flies, though George kept swatting at them.

Mindy put her arm around the mare's neck. "I don't have any more candy."

"That's all right. I've been eating sweet wild grass all morning. Did you have trouble last night?"

"Almost. But I got us out of it."

Her violet eyes, with long full lashes, considered George. Then her muzzle twitched, almost as though she wished to hide a smile. "Good," she said. "There will be more of it."

"We've decided," broke in Leigh, "to send you back."

"At all costs?" the spirit mare returned.

They nodded.

"Even to forfeit your mother?"

"Yes," said George and Leigh, but Mindy said, "What's forfeit mean?"

"It means to give up," Leigh told her.

Mindy frowned. "I don't want to give up Mom."

"Well, Rosebud doesn't mean that, exactly. What she means is, give up the chance to heal her, make her well, which she's told us she can't do."

"Oh." Mindy sounded unconvinced. She squeezed the mare's neck tighter. "Don't you think you should try, first? Like the Little Engine That Could?"

"Engine?" Now it was the mare's turn to be puzzled, and for a second, the conversation disintegrated into Leigh and George arguing and trying to explain what Mindy meant while Mindy kept interrupting and trying to explain the story. Rosebud let out a piercing whinny to restore order.

"I think," she said, "I have the idea. And, small Mindy, you are right, perhaps. I could try . . . but at great danger. That would summon the weevils for sure, and your mother may be too weak to make the journey and withstand the trial."

Mindy stood, blinking in bewilderment. "I don't understand."

"Trial?" repeated Leigh.

"Indeed. A spirit mare never gives out its powers to the undeserving."

"But I didn't—" George said, stretching out his newly healed hand, and the mare interrupted him.

"Didn't you? You wrestled with evil to protect your sister. How much more heroic do you think you should have been?"

His hand dropped as he said, "I . . . see. I think."

"Good. It's well you do." Rosebud shook her arched neck, and her white mane rippled in the sunlight, sending an aching, dazzling light into Leigh's eyes. She threw her head up. "How do you propose to send me back?"

"We're . . . not sure. If would help if we knew more about your Gate, and your world."

"Sit then, and I'll tell you what I remember, though it fades with every breath I take of this strange world."

"Fades?"

"Yes, dear. Even as I fade." The mare nuzzled Leigh's slender arm.

"What will happen?"

"I shall die, and then the balance will be forever corrupted, with weevils here."

"You can't fade! You have to go back!"

"If we can find the key, the power, the answer to what brought me here in the first place. Let me tell you of my country, and what it is like there. . . . "

"Dave? Dave, there's two gentlemen out here to see you. I think it's about Spirit Lake."

Dave looked up from a stack of two-by-fours at Mrs. Courtney, who looked pained to be having company with her house in such disarray. The tension returned with a snap, as he recognized the two men coming toward him, anger boiling in him that he quickly reined in, determined not to let them see it in him. Men such as he now faced liked to take emotion and twist it in their favor.

"Is this an official visit?" he asked.

"Yes, Mr. Stoner, it is. I'm Robinson and this is Pruett. We're from River Valley." The two of them sat down on a sawhorse. "You're in charge of the Spirit Lake area?" the first asked blandly, balancing a briefcase across his lap.

Mrs. Courtney frowned and walked back inside her house, past plywood sheeting that would soon become a wall.

"What did you have in mind?" What did they think they were doing, coming to a job site?

Pruett tapped the briefcase. "It's come to our attention that this valuable property has had some problems. There has been some talk, unofficially, that you've mismanaged the trust. Let runoff and pollution destroy the environmental structure."

Stoner gritted his teeth and stood, towering over them.

Pruett looked up, unafraid. "Our employer is prepared to take the property off your hands for a fair price, and to guarantee that the environment will be . . . cleaned up. This is preferable to taking action such as eminent domain, in which case you will lose both the property and the profit. The city guarantees us full cooperation. We're bringing in jobs and new population."

"I see." He smiled wryly at the cleverness of big business. "Gentlemen. I applaud the public spirit of your company. Since there are several worthwhile efforts in the area that could use your assistance, I feel it would be in my best interest to research the projects a little more thoroughly. Why don't I contact you in, say, two weeks?"

Their smiles tightened abruptly. "We won't be here in two weeks, Mr. Stoner."

"I see. That is awkward."

Pruett gathered the briefcase and stood up first. They both ignored the hand Stoner offered.

Then his opponent smiled again. "I suggest I meet with you again, at the end of the week?"

"I'd be foolish not to." Dave inclined his head and the two left. The air felt chilly in their wake.

A week. A week to save Spirit Lake. He saw Mrs. Courtney watching warily from a crack in the kitchen curtains and went over to ask to use the phone to call home.

Leigh watched as George jumped off the kitchen steps in one gangly, long-legged bound. She looked at his frown. "What is it?"

"Stoner says those two guys found him. He says if they show up here at the house, we're to lock the doors after we let Wolf out." He grinned.

But Leigh mirrored his earlier frown. "They're trouble."

Rosebud had been refreshing herself from the spring running along the shadow of the woods. She came trotting back. Leigh looked toward her, and her eyes misted over. The creature was definitely too beautiful to be part of this world, her spirituality too precious to let die because of them.

"We have to do something."

"I don't know how to undo it," George muttered.

"Maybe it's not you . . . maybe it's me."

George snorted. Leigh gave him a look of pure irritation. He sat, splitting twigs of hay with a broken thumbnail.

Then he looked up in sincerity. "I know," he said. "I know who might know."

"What?"

"This artist guy in town. At the gallery by the bus stop. He just might not think we're crazy. He knows about things inside of you, the hidden things. . . . "

"And how are we going to get in to town? You're not driving again."

He looked intently at Rosebud. "Four legs are faster than two."

Leigh followed the glance. "Oh, no. She'd never—"

"You don't know until you ask."

"Well, I'm not asking." Leigh crossed her arms. Not for him, she wouldn't. George always thought everything was his responsibility, everything since the car accident. Well, maybe it wasn't him. Maybe it was her. The mare was, after all, a unicorn and she was, well, a maiden. And if it was her, then it was up to her to find out how to help.

In the night, she lay still in bed until Mindy's gentle purring deepened, and her little mouth dropped open slightly, and she knew her sister dreamed of faraway places.

When that happened, she slipped quietly out from under the covers and took her still warm pillows and bolstered them against Mindy. Then she tucked her sister carefully into place.

She pulled her diary quietly out of her top drawer. It hadn't been written in very much in the two years since she'd gotten it. And most of it wasn't very important . . . except for the first and last page. On the first page, George had drawn a picture of their mother. And the last was tonight's entry. It was meant to tell George and Mindy where she'd gone and what she'd tried to do—if anything happened.

The pages fell open, and a lock of hair wafted to the bureau top. It lay curled, a honey-colored curve of fine hair. Leigh picked it up with a sudden, cutting ache of homesickness. She replaced it with a filament of white hair, hair that gleamed with a silvery purity—a strand from Rosebud. The spirit mare had let her clip it. "What can I do?" she whispered. She tore her mother's portrait from the diary and twisted it about the lock of her mother's hair. Then she tucked it into her shirt pocket, picked up her shoes, and tiptoed down the hall to the stairs.

The old house creaked with every movement. She was sure that Wolf would wake up and alarm everyone by barking. Instead, as she entered the kitchen, he merely opened one eye, looked at her, and went back to sleep with a doggish sigh. Leigh sat down and put her shoes on. She looked at the dog.

"What if there were weevils out there?" she queried.

He stretched in his sleep, unconcerned.

Outside came a soft, inquiring whicker. Leigh stood up and opened the door, squaring her shoulders against the night and the challenge ahead of her.

The spirit mare awaited her. Her hide shone like quicksilver and her aura rayed gold about her. No wonder Mindy still insisted she could see a horned unicorn. Leigh could almost see it herself.

Rosebud approached the steps. "All is well?"

"So far. Are you sure . . . you don't mind my riding?"

"Mount quickly. My being here may well bring the weevils."

"Right." Leigh took a deep breath and vaulted to the mare's back. She settled across the satiny hide and took a handful of mane.

Rosebud burned like a purging fire. It surged all the way through her soul. Leigh gasped with the astonishment of it, and then the moment passed, and she might have been riding any horse, though a fine-blooded one at that. Rosebud turned her head and eyed her.

"Well?"

"I'm ready."

The two cantered into the darkness. The mare moved under her with the fineness of well-knit muscle and bone, and Leigh realized with a little sadness that, after this, riding any horse would be ordinary. She gripped with her knees, but it wasn't necessary. She was being carried, borne, with a kind of royalty and dignity. She wasn't going to be allowed to fall.

They reached Spirit Lake close to midnight. Leigh

peered at her digital watch, which lit up with a faint glow. *The witching hour*, she thought. Rosebud halted by the shore, near a fairly even slope of beach.

"Now what do we do?"

"We heal you. That," said Leigh, pointing at the moon-washed lake, "is not just a product of my world. It's a piece of yours, too, it has to be, if you came from it. It's your Gate, and therefore you have power over it. You must go through it."

The silken hide twitched beneath her. Rosebud's tufted tail moved uneasily. "What if I cannot?"

"You can," Leigh answered fiercely. "We'll think about the rest later."

Then Rosebud caught her conviction and raised her head, and let loose with a ringing neigh across the waters. She plunged into the lake.

As she lowered her muzzle to the surface, the moon caught its golden brilliance, and Leigh gasped as it fired the pool around them. She sat in the sun's eye, in an aura of fire.

"Now, Rosebud! Now!" she cried, not thinking of what she would do if she was carried through with the white creature.

A rainbow shimmering opened before them. Rosebud raised her head and cried out, words Leigh could not understand, full of longing and hope. She thrust herself into deeper water as she sought the opening.

The lake tried to swallow them down. Leigh looked down and saw the dark waters reaching up as the mare began to swim. Howls pierced the sound of their splashing. Weevils had come, so soon, in answer to Rosebud's existence.

"I can't make it," the beast gasped. "It's closing again, without me!"

Leigh saw the rainbow mist waver. She reached into her pocket, just as the lake waters threatened to sweep her from Rosebud's back. It was the only hope she had. The plea for their mother had brought the mare to them. Now she would throw it back, hoping to free Rosebud. She threw the packet of hair into the mists.

With a boom, the lake exploded into a thousand colors, swallowing up the white elemental and her human rider.

THIRTEEN

GEORGE SLEPT BADLY. HE DREAMED of being surrounded by colossal blank sheets of paper, which sleek, deadly cars kept crashing through at incredible speeds, chasing him, their drivers with glowing crimson eyes. As the gigantic sheets of paper billowed out at him, he tried to draw on them. Stop signs, tunnels, whatever he could think of to divert the drivers intent on running him down.

First his hands would be paralyzed, unable to grip a pencil. Or the lead would break again and again. Or the sheet would flap in the wind like some immense sail, slapping him about the face, shouting, "Wake up! Wake up!"

George struggled awake to find a tiny hand stinging him on the cheek. "Mindy! Cut it out!"

She narrowed her eyes at him in the dimness of the bedroom. "Are you awake yet?"

"No. I always yell in my sleep. What do you want?" He rubbed at his gummy eyes, wondering how late it was. The house was still. Even Stoner's customary night thrashing could not be heard.

She put her finger to her lips, leaning closer. "Leigh's gone."

"What?" He sat bolt upright, the blankets jerked him down, and he wrestled to get clear of them. The fight tore the only three chest hairs he'd managed to grow yet out of his skin. He sat up, rubbing ruefully at his bare chest. "What do you mean, gone?"

Mindy had a book under her arm. She pushed it at George. It was Leigh's diary and it had been creased open to the last entry. He rolled out of bed, went to the window, and read it by moonlight. His heart sank. "Oh, great. This's all my fault."

"It is?" Mindy's soft, furry eyebrows rose until they tangled with the fringe of her dark bangs. "How come?"

"Because. Because I did something really wrong and it keeps coming out in my drawings. And . . . and that's making all this stuff happen. I don't know how to explain it, Mindy." His throat went tight on him.

"Like writing bad words on walls and the subway?"

"Sort of. I mean, I drew the weevils and there they were . . . I don't know how." George closed the diary and put it down. "We've got to find Leigh. And I've got to find out what's happening to me."

There was a jangle in Mindy's fingers as she held up her hand. "I've got the car keys," she said hopefully. "And my book."

Downtown looked deserted at one in the morning. Summer night dew had already begun to dampen the lawns of the little frame and brick houses lining the road before the row of shops began. George drove really slowly, unhappy to be at the wheel, Mindy slumped against him, lulled half-asleep by the drive. Home, the streets would still have been crowded, full of empty people seeking something to fill them up. And George didn't think they were looking for a good Chinese take-out. No. They were looking for something more elusive, something deadlier, something much more complicated. Drugs, sex, whatever. He was glad he was gone for the summer.

Still, a sense of menace trembled in the air as he got

out and handed Mindy down. The bus station was closed and gated up. The art gallery looked a little dingy, the streetlight in front of it dark, broken, and still. It looked like a prime candidate for tear-down and replacement. Mindy said, "Is this the place?" She pressed her nose against the front window hard enough to rattle the glass as she looked in. "Nice pictures."

"Yeah." George craned his head back. Unless he missed his guess, the upstairs was an apartment. He was not sure if the gallery owner lived up there but he had to take his chances. "Come on. Let's go wake up a perfect stranger."

This would be snow country in the wintertime. The stairs inside were old, brown, heavily glazed linoleum with a finish like yellowed glass. They reflected the children as they took the steps up. George took a deep breath and knocked briskly on the door.

The door jerked inward so quickly that he fell forward half a step and Mindy let out a high, piercing squeak. The Asian gallery owner glared fiercely above a pair of black silk pajamas embroidered with a curling silver dragon, and a nunchaku—heavy sticks chained together—hung from his hand. "What do you want?"

Mindy dropped her book with a thud. It fluttered open.

"I—uh—" George fumbled for words. "I came for help."

The moon face looked at him solemnly. "I remember you, boy. You need help stealing something? You set off my alarm downstairs."

Mindy trembled at his flank. George put a hand back to steady her. Knowing he had to defend her gave him strength. "She didn't mean to. She was looking in the front windows. Are the . . . are the police coming?"

The embroidered dragon rippled as its wearer laughed dryly. "Not hardly. I am on my own."

George swallowed hard. "I've got to talk to you about your paintings."

The man slowly closed his eyes and opened them again. "You do not look dangerous. All right, come in."

Sun Ling sat with the book spread across his lap. Mindy had finished her tea, heavily laced with milk and sugar, and laid her head down on the small drafting table that doubled as a dining table. George curled on a large silk cushion of red and gold. Something in the fabric with green eyes sparkled at him.

The Asian artist had been listening solemnly, without interruption, until George spoke his last words and sat, totally drained. The man stroked fine fingers over the book and its pages.

"That is not everything you should be telling me. You have secrets, George."

George stiffened. Sun made a tiny smile. "But it is not for me to know them. I only know you have them because why should such a young man be so frightened of the darkness in his soul . . . be so worried that your drawings are the gateway for something so dire as these . . . weevils. My homeland was in war. We fight still. I dream of fire and smoke and bullets. What do you dream of?"

George tightened his lips. He thought he'd said enough.

Sun took a deep breath. "This is very fine paper," he said. "It's rice paper, did you know that? Very fine. And your drawings do it justice. This paper takes me back to my youth. We had paper like this for our New Year's prayers, to send our wishes to Buddha."

"Prayer paper?"

"Yes." Sun whispered his fingertips over the page again. "Yes. In fact—"

An eerie howl yodeled somewhere downstairs. George jumped to his feet. Mindy's head came up, her eyes wide.

"They're here," she said.

"What are here?"

A heavy thump on the roof punctuated Sun's question. The slender man shoved the book back at George and got to his feet. He grabbed the nunchaku lying on the couch.

George thought he could hear hot, sizzling growls. His breath rattled in his throat. "I told you—"

Sun paced the floor of the apartment. Footfalls sounded above. Whether he traced them, or they tracked the man, George could not tell. The artist waved his hand. "Go. I'll hold them."

"They'll be downstairs. Between us and the car." George's forehead began to sprout sweat. He gripped the book. His secrets. Dark secrets.

Sun looked piercingly at him. "An artist uses the vision. He does not let the vision use him. Protect your sister. Go!"

"You believe me?"

"Yes! But that doesn't matter. You must believe in yourself." Sun came to a halt. The roof began to pound.

George looked upward. Were they strong enough to tear away the roofing? Would they come through? He grabbed Mindy. Howls rose above them. "Run for it!"

Something stung him in the fingers as he caught up his sister. She had a sketching pencil, very sharp, in her hand. He grabbed it and fished the car keys out of his jeans pocket. They ran for the stairs. He heard Sun yell in defiance behind them. Snarls answered.

He braced his shoulder against the outside door and looked down at Mindy. "You've got to stay with me and run your fastest."

She looked up in innocence. "No, I don't."

"Yes, you do. Or they'll get you."

"Draw a picture."

George fought a breath down. "I . . . can't . . . draw . . . us . . . out of this."

"Try it."

Something hurled at the door. It came open, thumping against him. He threw his weight back and the door slammed shut again. He looked upstairs. He could hear furniture sliding in Sun's apartment. They had no future going backward. And he was afraid to go outside.

Mindy tugged at his hand. "Hurry."

George opened the book. He licked his lips. A blank page the gateway between his soul and reality . . .

Mindy, safe.

He began to sketch her sitting in the car, buckled in, window beside her up and door locked. Her eyes wide . . .

The outside door rattled again. Then, a massive blow knocked him aside, sent him rolling into the wall. The book skidded across the floor one way, the pencil the other. He lay gasping for breath.

Something dark and furry swept up Mindy. She let out a surprised squeak. Then the door boomed shut again, and George lay all alone in the stairwell.

FOURTEEN

GEORGE SCRAMBLED FOR THE book and lunged at the door. He broke it open and skidded outside, but the alleyway between the buildings was empty. Not even the thin echoing scream of Mindy's fear remained.

"Damn." He pivoted on his heel and raced around front, to the car, cursing with every pounding step. What would they do with her? Would they kill her or . . . was it him they wanted? Would they use her as bait?

Something shadowy moved inside the cab of the four-wheeler. He flung himself at the door handle as something hot and smelly snarled at his heels. The door lock caught, then gave way. A surprised, wide-eyed Mindy watched as he bolted inside and locked the doors.

They stared at one another. "What are you doing in here?"

"I screamed and kicked and it dropped me," Mindy panted. "Go, George! Go!"

The vehicle rocked as a weevil charged it. Metal shuddered. Clawed fingers skritched against the window glass. Slaver was flung from a snarling grin. George jabbed the keys into the ignition and started the car with a roar. The tires squealed as he pulled away with a scorching start. Something heavy thudded in their wake.

George's whole body throbbed. He looked at Mindy. The door was locked on her side. He automatically locked the remaining doors. "Kicked and screamed, huh?"

"And bit," she said. "Like I used to in preschool and Mom said I couldn't." She made a face. "They're hairy."

He'd drawn her here, safe. Had he made it happen . . . or had he only known it could have happened. Wished it would happen. Could he use this to find Leigh? Save their mother? Sweat poured down his face. He didn't know!

He took a deep breath. "Mindy, we've got to tell Stoner. If Leigh's not back when we get there, we've got to find her."

His little sister began to cry, silently. He put a hand on her shoulder. "It's okay now," he said.

"I kn-know. But I'm scared, anyway."

She was still crying when they pulled up at the rustic house. Lights blazed from the windows. Either Leigh had come home and roused their host, or he'd woken and found everyone gone. George pulled Mindy from the car and walked her in, using her as a shield against the man's anger.

Dave Stoner and Wolf reared in the doorway.

"Where have you been?"

"Where's Leigh?" George asked.

The man's face creased in puzzlement. "I thought you had her again."

George shook his head. "I went looking for her."

Mindy turned her sobbing face to Stoner. "She's gone!" she hiccoughed.

"Leigh?"

Mindy nodded, after stuffing her hand into her mouth to quiet her sobs.

Stoner turned on his heel. He could be heard taking the stairs at a furious leap, calling Leigh's name.

After long moments, he returned. The man had evidently slept in his clothes. The work shirt and jeans were all rumpled, and his dark brown hair with the gray at the temples was rumpled, too. He gave a tired smile.

"Let's talk about this."

George nodded, and took Mindy's hand. "We need the journal. Then you have to take a look at your car. The dent and the scratches in the window might convince you."

To Stoner's credit, he only blanched a little at the word "dent" and said nothing as George and Mindy came to the kitchen table, diary in hand. George started to talk.

Stoner listened to his every word, and read the journal, and looked at the strand of hair lying across the tabletop. It shone, even in the bright light of the kitchen.

"So you think Leigh took the spirit mare and went back to the lake with her."

"That's what she wrote."

"What in the hell were you kids thinking of? Or any of us? I don't know if this is real or—"

"Or what?" George said softly. "We wanted healing for Mom. Don't you understand that? Ifs and maybes and coulds are all we get from the doctors. Well, that's not good enough! We want to know for sure."

The man sat quietly, then answered, "I know you do." He moved slightly in the chair as though it were uncomfortable for him. "Why the lake?"

"Leigh thought maybe the old Indian magic might help. So we brought the unicorn through. I don't know if I summoned it or . . . what."

"Carrie always loved that lake," Stoner said, remembering. "Before we were married, and then, later, after my grandparents had died and left it to me, and I'd just gotten back from Nam . . . we came here for a few weeks while we were deciding. . . ."

"Deciding what?" Mindy asked clearly.

They looked at one another, the man and the little girl. He reached out and smoothed down her ruffled hair.

"Whether or not we were going to stay married."

"Oh."

Dave tapped his strong, tanned fingers on the table. Then, abruptly, he reached for the strand of hair. There was a hiss, like cold water in a hot frying pan. With a yell, he dropped it. George looked at him in astonishment as Mindy gathered up the lock.

Dave blew on his fingers.

Mindy's face paled and she said, "Shadow-touched."

George stared, his mouth open.

Dave gingerly sucked his fingertip. "No," the man answered. "But the unicorn is only for the innocent, or so the legends say."

George blushed furiously.

Dave pushed his chair back, balancing it on the back rungs. "I wasn't sure if I believed it." He took a deep breath. "Now, I think the next thing to do is drive out to Spirit Lake and see what we can see."

"Uh, Dave—"

They looked at one another and then George swallowed. "If you have a gun or something, I think we'd better take it. The weevils are just as real."

Stoner nodded abruptly. "Then get Mindy dressed and let's go."

Spirit Lake was dark and foreboding, with a heavy mist lying over it that belied the summer night and calm. George and Mindy sat shivering in the front seat of the car as Stoner got out. He tramped the shore a moment, then leaned back in.

"I don't like the looks of that fog. It's not natural."

"It wasn't there last night."

Mindy pointed. "It's got rainbows!"

They stared. Indeed, a prismatic sheen played over the

mist from time to time. George stirred, uneasily aware that the longer they sat in the wilderness, the more likely they were to attract weevils.

Stoner cupped his hands and shouted. "Leigh! Leigh!"

A startled bird winged from the brush along the lake, crying eerily, before it wheeled and disappeared over the water. Stoner stood, listening and waiting.

Mindy waited a long time, then said, "Do you think the weevils got them?"

"No!" George took a deep breath, "No, I don't. Listen, why don't you lie down and go to sleep or something."

She gave him a withering look, pursed her lips, and stared at Stoner, who was shouting again.

A faint, quavering sound answered him. The hair on the back of George's neck rose. Stoner turned, his heel grinding in the dirt.

"What was that?"

George shook his head, answering, "I don't know."

"Come out here and listen with me."

They stood. The lake lapped gently at the shoreline. Then it came again. Faint. Very far away. George thought his heart was going to stop when he recognized it.

It was Leigh, crying for their mother.

He elbowed Stoner, but Stoner had already deciphered it for himself. He cupped his hands. "Leigh! Where are you?"

"Heeeere! Inside the Gate. We're . . . stuck!"

Stoner began stripping off his jacket and George grabbed his arm. "What are you going to do?"

"Someone's got to go in after her."

"You don't understand! That's—that's like an alternate world or something. We don't know how she got in there."

The man stopped. "Then who would?"

"Maybe . . . me. But I can't . . . I can't . . . I have to talk to Mom." George answered slowly. "There's something important she's got to know. Sun Ling said there was a darkness in my mind. That I have secrets." He looked up. "But I can only tell Mom."

An unreadable look passed over the man's face, and then he said, "There's a pilot at the county airport who owes me a favor. I think it's time your mom found out what's going on here."

"But Leigh—"

Stoner grasped George's shoulder tightly. "Pray the mist holds." He shouted back at the lake, "Hold on, Leigh! We'll be back!"

His voice echoed in the dark stillness. If Leigh answered, it was lost in the wind.

FIFTEEN

THE NURSE PATTED HER GENTLY on the arm and said, "I'll call a cab. Why don't you wait in the lounge?"

Caroline sighed and let what was left of her seemingly boneless body drop into a heavily cushioned chair. She clenched her teeth, tilted her head back, and let the waves of relief wash over her. She'd gotten through another treatment. The nurse's shoes squeaked against the highly polished floor as she walked off. It would be at least an hour before the cab would show. It was a ritual between the nursing staff and Caroline. She was being detained on purpose, subtly, so that if she felt ill, they could assist her. But they also knew her stubbornness in that she hated to spend even an extra minute at the clinic, so they would pass the time waiting for the "tardy" cab to arrive.

With her head back and her eyes closed, she drowsed a little, then woke, her heart thumping, for she had dreamed of that man following her again. She'd seen him several times. It frightened her. Was she being stalked? If so, why? And who could help her?

Caroline opened her eyes and stroked her face lightly. Her skin felt clammy. Perhaps she had imagined all but the first encounter, but even as she told herself that, she knew she was lying to herself. She had seen him—it—at least twice. It could be the medicine they were giving her for the nausea. She'd meant to ask the doctor about that. She lay limply a second, wondering if she had the strength to get up and go back to the nursing station and ask.

She could see herself. *Pardon me, but does this stuff make me see men in business suits with hands like claws and glowing red eyes?*

A hand dropped on her shoulder from behind. "Carrie?"

Her scream stuck in her throat. It came out like a strangling gasp and she wrenched away from the hand, balling up her own into fists, and prepared to scream, for real this time, for a nurse.

The man dodged back, concern etched into his deeply tanned face. Then her mouth dropped open in surprise.

"Dave!"

"Are you—are you all right?"

"Yes, except that I—I thought I was seeing things again." She stood up. "What are you doing here? Where are the children? Are they all right? What's wrong?"

His gaze didn't quite meet hers as he said, "They're fine. Listen, I've brought a private plane down, and drove in to see you. You're done here for the week, right?"

"Yes." She smiled thinly. The surge of adrenaline that had brought her to her feet threatened to run out and leave her swaying. "Once a week is about all I can take."

"Then come back with me. Visit for a couple of days. There's nothing holding you here. The kids are, well, homesick—and they've had a rough time adjusting."

"Is it Mindy? She called. I've been trying to call back—I know she's been upset." He didn't answer, and she picked up her purse. "All right. I'd like a few days of peace and quiet and clean air."

"Good. Let's go get you packed."

She took his arm. The nurse saw them coming out of the lounge and called out, "Mrs. Walsh? Are you going now?"

"Yes, thank you. When the cab comes, please tell them it's not necessary."

The nurse smiled thinly. "See you next week."

Outside the hospital doors, both of them took a deep breath, then laughed at each other.

"I can't stand the smell," Dave said.

"Me neither." She paused. She felt the tenseness in his arm. It was still very hard for her to face him, and she wondered if he felt that way, too. "What's wrong? I know there's something you're not telling me."

He flashed her a half smile. "It'll wait. Let's get you packed and home, first."

She thought of reminding him that it was his home, not hers, then thought better of it. "I think I'd better warn you, though, I get really airsick now."

"Consider me warned." He pulled his arm tighter around her, and she thought fleetingly how welcome his warm strength felt.

Caroline knew that something troubled Stoner. She bit her lip, wondering what had happened between him and the children, but she kept to the polite conversation offered, aware that a stranger piloted the plane. Whatever was between her and Dave was private, and should be kept that way.

In the car, driving through the woods and green-brown fields, he said only that Leigh was in trouble.

"What kind of trouble?"

He hesitated. "I think that should wait until we get home. George can help explain it."

Her heart skipped a beat. Her hands trembled as she searched her purse for her pills, and gripped the vial tightly in her fist. As they turned off the side road, she felt strange. She felt fifteen years, no, make that twenty years younger, barely older than George himself, when she'd first come to this wilderness. Already engaged, soon to be married.

She rolled the car window down. It was morning still here, and though it was going to be a hot summer day, a slight breeze stirred the heavy evergreen boughs and the hardwoods. It smelled heavenly. Her heartbeat steadied. Then she saw the house. Curtains rippled at the front windows.

"Is that—is that Mindy?"

Stoner frowned. Then he grinned. "I think so."

Her throat ached. How she'd missed them, and it had only been six days. She never should have sent them away!

Mindy barreled out of the door and threw herself at Caroline even as she straightened up from the car seat. It took all of her frail strength to absorb the blow. She hugged her daughter back, tightly.

George stood over her. He blushed, then hugged her, too. For a moment, she could barely see through the hot, stinging tears that flooded her eyes. Then she brushed them off.

"Now tell me what's happened to Leigh?"

George looked away from her to Stoner, and something unseen passed between them. George opened his mouth to answer, but Mindy interrupted him.

"Did the weevils get you, Mommy? Did they scare you?"

"Weevils?" Caroline leaned over, puzzled. "But, Mindy—" Then she stopped dead. "What kind of weevils, honey?"

"They look like men, but they're not. George says they're werewolves. And they wear suits like Daddy used to wear, and hats, y'know, and their eyes are all hot and red—"

Caroline thought she was going to faint.

Stoner gripped her suddenly from behind. "Let's get her in the house. George, get the bags."

Mindy looked up. "Mommy—you're all white."

Stoner swung his arms under Caroline and lifted her up. "Go open the door, Mindy."

"Sure, but—what's wrong with Mommy?"

"I'll be all right, honey. Just—just sick." Caroline closed her eyes and let her head fall against Dave's shoulder as he strode into the house, carrying her.

Half an hour and two cups of hot tea later, she felt stronger and sat up on the couch. She looked at Dave. He sat, with his big hands balanced on his kneecaps, watching her closely. George was tense. He kept pacing back and forth in front of the fireplace, while Mindy sat at her side, curled up in a ball, desperately unhappy. Stoner had kept her shushed.

Caroline put down her empty teacup. "All right. What's happening?"

"I don't think you'd believe us if we told you."

She wet her lips. "Then let me start. Mindy, I've seen your weevils. Or, I think I have. And I know that's not possible, but there it is. One of them has been following me."

Mindy shot a triumphant look at George. "See! I told you Mommy was in trouble."

"So what does this have to do with Leigh? Where is she?"

"We don't know, for sure," Dave said. His gaze measured her as she panicked momentarily, fought it, and then sat, sorting out her feelings. "I have no explanation for what's going on here, except that it is, and you're involved. The children have seen a unicorn, from the book George drew, and it comes from another place and time, through a gate of some sort. And the weevils also come through this gate. They're here because the white mare was here—"

"Light and dark had to be balanced," interjected George.

Caroline looked at them. "That's not possible."

"It is, too," Mindy said. She held up a silken thread of hair. "And this is part of Rosebud's mane. Leigh clipped it off, to save it."

Even as Dave said, "I wouldn't do that," she reached for it. A fiery pain lashed through her fingertips and she dropped it on the floor. She stared at it in horror even as the burn throbbed on her fingers. "What in God's name is it?"

"We told you," Stoner said calmly. "It's from the creature's mane. I think it's real, Carrie. I've never seen anything like it before. It's more than horsehair. It has a luminescence—and it burned me, too."

She blew on her fingers, soothing them. Mindy picked it up and tucked it back into the book she held in her lap. Caroline recognized Leigh's diary.

The woman sat in shocked silence another moment longer. Then she burst out, "My God! What has happened to Leigh?"

"We're . . . not sure. She's with the white mare. You see, the children tried to keep it here because they wanted to use it to heal you. But the beast said that it couldn't, and that it wasn't meant to be here, and that the Gate had to be fixed so it could return. Leigh took it—"

"Her," Mindy interrupted. "Rosebud's a her!"

Stoner glared at her, then the corners of his mouth softened. "Right. Her. Leigh took her to the lake to try and fix the Gate. And, as near as I can tell, they're stuck there."

"In the lake?" Then Caroline's face changed. "Which lake?"

"Spirit Lake."

She moaned very softly, and clenched her hands in her lap. He looked at the pallor of her face, and feared for her.

"Are you all right?"

"I don't understand any of this!" She sat, hunched over. "This isn't happening."

"Believe it, Mom. It's real." George walked over and took her hands in his. "It's like science fiction or something. Rosebud really does exist in another world. Somehow, I drew her. And the others."

She let her hands, hot and fevered, rest in his slightly cool ones. She looked up at her son, realizing that he seemed very adult in that moment. She took her hands away. "I used to drive out to the lake. When things were . . . bad . . . between us." Her gaze flickered to Stoner. "I would sit and pray, and dream in the sun." She took a deep breath. "How are we going to find Leigh?"

Stoner's lips tightened. "I don't know." He stood up. "I'm going back there after her. I'll do what she did."

"But what did she do?"

He grinned without humor. "She rode a unicorn into the lake, and tossed a lock of your hair in before her. At least, that's what she wrote down in her journal."

Caroline put a hand to her scarf-turbaned head. She smiled wryly. "Well, if it's hair you need, it's coming out by the handfuls."

George stood tensely by the back door. "I want to go with you."

"No. I want you to stay here with your mother and sister."

They eyed each other. Then Stoner added, "Look, you've seen the weevils. There could be trouble. Your mother's not strong enough to face it if there is. And if it's your drawings, you can't go disappearing on us. You may be the only thing that can bring us back."

"But what if—"

"I don't come back? Call Johannsen. Don't tell him what's going on, just have him drive you out to the lake. Agreed? In the meantime, you talk to your mother. You said you had things to tell her."

"All right." Reluctantly, George let Stoner pass. Wolf

started to follow him out, but the man pointed and said, "No! Stay."

The dog let out a low whine and returned to the kitchen, where he pressed against George's legs.

Stoner looked up. The sky boiled with clouds, and a wind whistled through the farmyard. He turned his collar up. In his pocket was another page of the book, folded over a braid of white mane and Caroline's hair. George had done a hasty sketch of Dave and Leigh coming together, with Rosebud and a nebulous gate in the background. He looked back to George. "Wish me luck."

"Luck," the tall boy said.

Mindy pushed around him and bolted out the door and threw herself on the man. Stoner picked her up.

"Be careful," she said solemnly. Then, "I love you!" with a hug, and then she wiggled down and was back in the house.

Speechless, Stoner looked after her. Then he shrugged into his denim jacket and went to the car.

George went in to the living room after locking the door. His mother had returned to the windows and stood by the front curtains, watching the car leave. He heard her whisper, "Please let him bring back my little girl."

"What are you doing, Mom? Praying?"

She looked to him. "Yes," she answered simply.

He licked his lips. Outside, the unusual storm continued to build. A gust of wind hit the house. Was it his imagination, or did the building shudder under the blow? The air outside turned dark, as though it were nearly nighttime. Twilight, he thought.

From far away, he heard the howls on the wind. The hair rose on the back of George's neck.

"Mindy! Run through the house. Make sure all the windows and shutters are locked." He swallowed hard, suddenly afraid, remembering the grooves cut into Mindy's bedroom window.

"What is it?" his mother asked.

"I think we're in trouble," George answered slowly.

The howls began again. They were headed in their direction.

SIXTEEN

MINDY BOUNDED DOWN THE stairs, her face flushed and out of breath. "All done," she announced. "What's happening?"

The air outside had darkened with clouds, but a sulfurous, yellowish glow pulsated through it. Her mother turned away from the windows, saying, "I don't know. It's almost as if it were tornado weather or something."

"Or something." George strode back in from the kitchen. He ran his fingers through his hair, leaving a light brown fringe standing up. Mindy giggled at him and he glared at her. "Don't touch the shotgun. It's loaded."

"All right."

"Is that necessary?" asked Caroline.

He shrugged. "I don't know, Mom. I hope we don't have to find out."

A sharp *caaaw* interrupted him.

"What's that?" Mindy plunged to the window, looking. "Crows! The sky is full of them!"

"What?"

The two of them joined her. Wheeling out from the edge of the woods, a cloud of black crows arose. They circled the barn and then came at the house, dozens of them, yellow eyes gleaming malevolently.

George grabbed Mindy and Caroline backed away from the window as the birds threw themselves at the house. Hundreds of wings beating, talons scratching. Black feathers flew in the wind. Their eyes glowed. Beaks scratched and pecked. The roof thundered under their blows.

Caroline looked at the fireplace. "Close the flue, George! The lever there, to the right!"

Dragging Mindy with him, George did as he was told, hand shaking. The lever fought him, then clanked shut as it should. A loud, evil caw rattled down the fireplace, then the sounds muffled.

Wolf loped up and down the stairs. He barked sharply, ears pricked.

"I hope the windows hold," George muttered.

A thousand drumsticks rattled the house. The squawking and cawing of the crows filled the air until George thought he was going to be deafened and never hear again. Suddenly, there was silence.

Caroline gingerly picked aside the curtains. She gasped at the sight. Dozens of crows littered the ground. A storm of dark feathers blackened the driveway and flowerbeds. They had literally battered themselves to death against the building, dying with their beaks open and their talons stretched. The remainder had gone, as suddenly as they came.

"Holy cow," Mindy breathed.

Her mother shuddered and drew her in. The curtains shut away the carnage outside.

The wind came up again. It whistled and shook the beams of the house. George looked up as though he could see an unseen enemy. Wolf whined and shoved his nose into George's hand.

He heard the howls again. Closer. And from the barn, a

sudden bleating. The goats! The kids were out there, at the mercy of whatever was coming to assault them.

He went to the back door and looked out, tentatively. His mother followed after.

"I'm going out."

"You can't!"

"I have to. I can't leave the kids in the barn, unprotected." He picked up the shotgun and gave it to her. "The safety clicks off here. Just aim it and pull the trigger. Brace yourself, though."

She wrinkled her nose. "I'm not going to shoot this."

"If a weevil grabs me, you're my only hope." George braced himself and unlocked the kitchen door.

He had to grunt and push to shove it open. Crows were piled on the back steps. One of them twitched and stabbed at his ankle. "Ouch!" George cried, and kicked it away, where it flopped on the bodies of its mates. Beyond, the driveway was mostly clear. He took a deep breath and plunged out of the safety of the house.

The goats were joyously excited to see him. The whites of their eyes showed as they rolled them, and butted up against his legs. They were scared, too, without knowing why.

"Think you're scared now," George muttered. "Just wait." He grabbed their bottles out of the old fridge and stuck them in his jacket pockets, then grabbed one under each arm.

The goats bucked and fought, but he held them tightly. "Come on, now! You're coming with me!"

He moved back across the gravel, avoiding black patches of feathered bodies, head down, concentrating on what he was doing.

He never saw the snarling form until it leapt, and hit, swinging him around, tearing a goat from under his arm. George screamed and kicked out as glowing red eyes turned around to face him. No suit. No hat. Just furred evil waiting for him.

His kick caught the weevil in the throat. It staggered back, hot and stinking. Its fangs clashed as it grabbed for the kid's neck. George picked up the terrified goat. Its blood soaked through to his arm, warm and sticky, as he staggered up the back steps, yelling, "Let me in!"

His mother opened the door and he leapt through, screaming, "Shut it! Shut it!"

Wolf sprang to the opening. The beasts snarled and snapped at each other and locked together. George grabbed a dish towel and wrapped it around the bleeding kid. His mother stood frozen, the shotgun lying on the kitchen table next to her as Wolf fought in the doorway.

Snarl and leap. Slash and tear. The two fought, and outside, George could hear another growling begin.

"Shoot! Pick it up and shoot!"

She couldn't move. It was as though she were carved out of ice, or stone, frozen to the floor. Mindy let out a piercing scream as Wolf was dragged slowly across the doorway.

George grabbed the shotgun himself and followed. The dark, furry weevil and black-and-silver dog curved together, around and around. He sighted. There was no way he could avoid hitting Wolf, too. But he couldn't let the weevil get in. His vision blurred and he pulled the trigger quickly, before he could think about it longer.

The blast knocked him head over heels, and a sharp yelp was cut off abruptly. Caroline gasped, then pulled the dog's body back inside and slammed the door shut.

The dog got to his feet unsteadily, his jaws and coat stained with a slimy-looking blood. George blinked. "Wolf!"

The dog collapsed across his knees, tail thumping. Except for a gash or two, the dog was unhurt. He lay over George, panting.

Boom! The backdoor trembled under the assault, but it held. They held their breath, listening to the snarling and growling outside. Something was dragged off the back steps. A moment's silence, then unsavory noises followed.

Mindy gagged. "I think they're eating each other," she said unsteadily.

Caroline moved quickly. She shoved the butcher block against the door with a grunt. George helped her. It braced the back door. She looked around. "What about the windows?"

"Stoner spent all night putting up storm windows. That's a double thickness. Besides," and George smiled weakly, "they're from another world. I don't think they know much about glass. At least, I hope not."

Mindy said, "The baby goat's bleeding."

George went to them, sinking on his knees. He dabbed the dish towel at the cut. "It's scabbing up already. It'll be fine." He remembered the bottles in his pocket. "Why don't you feed 'em?"

"Not in here," Caroline said. "In the living room." She picked up the shotgun and moved past them.

Wolf stopped licking his cuts and followed them, stiffly, with a low whine. George hesitated. Was all this coming out of the darkness of his soul? How could he ever tell his mother? How could he ever change things? He let out a groan of despair, then followed.

For a few minutes, the only thing that could be heard was the greedy slurping of the goats. Then George became aware that something ran across the roof. It growled down the chimney. Caroline looked up. She shuddered. Her scarf turban went a little crooked.

Mother and son's eyes met.

She said, "I'm not just going to sit here and wonder if Leigh's all right. I'm calling the Johannsens."

"What are you going to do?"

"I'm going to ask them to come over and let me take their car."

"But what about—"

"All of this?" She shook her head. "I don't know. But I think it's us the creatures want. I don't think they'll stay here once we leave."

"I'll call," George said. "I know the number."

Inga answered. She sounded concerned. "What's happening out your way, George? The weather looks bad."

"It sure does. And we've got trouble with that—that wild dog pack. We're here alone. Can you drive out and let us take the car? Dave's at Spirit Lake."

"Alone? Mr. Johannsen is in the city. I'll leave the girls and bring the station wagon over."

"Thanks. And—uh—be careful."

"I will."

She rang off and George hung up.

They gathered in the living room. Every now and then, there was a snarling at the living room windows. A red aura seemed to burn through the curtains, as though the weevils could see them anyway. The back door shook as a body hurtled against it. George hugged his knees to his chest, sitting on the floor near the staircase, listening to the siege.

The weevils and Wolf heard the Johannsen car before they heard the crunch of tires on the gravel. Wolf sprang to his feet with an excited bark. He knew neighbors when he heard them, and his tail waved.

"That's her!" George got to his feet. He went to the back door and looked out. Inga drove the car very slowly near the back steps. He could see Tom sitting in the front seat with her, the barrel of a rifle in his hands.

"They brought a rifle," George reported.

"What about the—the weevils?"

"I don't see them."

Wolf's head turned to the back, to the empty pasture and woods, and he growled softly.

The station wagon door swung open and Tom Johannsen eased his stocky sixteen-year-old body out. Inga got out, and she carried a handgun.

A blurry shape moved behind the barn. George shoved aside their barricade and fumbled at the kitchen door lock.

Tom cried out, raised the rifle, and shot. The beast went tumbling in the shadows.

As George threw open the door, the weevils ran, doglike, across the pasture and disappeared into the fringe of the woods. Inga grimaced as she stepped over the unrecognizable carcasses near the back steps.

She clucked, "Poor kids. You got trouble. Tom, you'd better call the sheriff and tell him we got the dog pack here." She hugged Mindy. Her raw-boned face paused thoughtfully as she spotted Caroline.

Caroline held out her hand. "I'm the children's mother."

"Of course you are. Dave didn't tell me he was bringing you up for a few days."

Before either woman could say anything further, Tom said, "I'm going to take a look at what I shot behind the barn."

"No," George blurted out. "That is . . . the dogs didn't go far. You won't be safe."

"No," Inga seconded. "Go call the sheriff like I told you to." She pressed the station wagon keys into Caroline's hand. "What's wrong?"

"Leigh . . . Leigh found that old mare and took her riding, to Spirit Lake," George stammered.

Caroline finished smoothly, "Dave's gone after her, and with this weather, and the dogs . . ."

Inga nodded. "Never seen anything like this. Crows outside littering the ground . . . I don't blame you being worried. We'll stay." She looked to Wolf. "He's been hurt."

"He fought one of the dogs when I was bringing the goats in."

"I'll get him fixed up. You two go ahead."

Mindy blurted out, "I wanna go!"

"No, honey. You'd better stay here."

Her face pinched up, and George started to say, "Mindy—"

She turned and bolted from the kitchen. Her footsteps echoed up the stairs.

Inga sighed. "She doesn't know me so well. Maybe she'd better stay with you. . . ."

"But the drive." Caroline stopped. She sagged into a kitchen chair. "Mrs. Johannsen, I don't know what you make of all this. . . ."

"We heard the tornado watch over the TV. Sometimes birds get caught in them, like they did here, and get sucked in. It can't be very pleasant for you. We'll have the sheriff's department come and go after the dogs, and then we'll get the rest of this mess cleaned up. Don't you worry."

Her sturdy Swedish advice was broken by Mindy's return. She clutched the Rosebud book under one arm.

"I'm going," she announced. "Or I'm telling."

George took a step toward her, but his mother stopped him. "All right, honey," she said. "Although you'll be safer here."

"Don't want to be safer. I want to find Leigh."

The three of them ran to the station wagon while Tom covered them with the rifle. A howl started from the edge of the woods and broke off sharply. Caroline started the car and tore out of the circular driveway.

"Which way am I going?"

George reminded her, then added, "And if you don't feel like driving, Mom—I can."

She gave him a look and said nothing further as Mindy added, "Yeah, he's done it already."

Caroline sucked in her breath sharply as she looked in the rearview mirror.

"What is it?"

She watched the furry pack break out of the woods and hit the asphalt, running after them. "They're coming after us. How far or fast can they run?"

"I don't know," George answered. He looked out the back window. "Just watch out for a red-and-black car, low and sleek. That's real trouble."

Her mouth pinched white at the corners, Caroline floored the accelerator.

SEVENTEEN

THE SUN SHIMMERED HOTLY OVER the lake. As Dave eased the four-wheel drive into position, he scanned its shores. Few people came out to the lake now. Fishing was poor, swimming banned. And even though Spirit Lake was a pretty lake, picnickers preferred to go elsewhere, where the pall of dying was not so apparent. He had an eerie image of Caroline walking this shore as she had twenty years ago . . . Leigh an echo of her youth and beauty before divorce, remarriage, widowhood, and cancer.

The image faced him, saying, "Just tell me when it is you're going to stop fighting the war alone and let me help . . . and I'll tell you that I can stay."

"Carrie . . ." His voice faded. The lakeside was still and empty.

He stepped out of the vehicle. A heavy mist still hung over the center, a grayish, ugly-looking fog. Even as he watched, it seemed to catch and dazzle the summer sun. A gate to everywhere—or nowhere? Or was he still lying in his own bed, agonizing over his decision to take Caroline's children for the summer, in a cold sweat over her mortal illness? Was he still fighting shadows in his dreams?

An eerie howling broke into his thoughts. Dave craned his neck and looked about the lake and surrounding woods, not seeing anything, but not liking what he heard. He bent over and picked up a fallen tree branch, a good five-foot length, and swung it like a baseball bat. Men could die in their sleep, he thought. Who knew if it was because something had attacked them in their dreams or not?

He gripped the pine bough tightly. Dead, but not dry, still tough and flexible. He could beat a few of Mindy's weevils off with it.

He walked down the rocky shore to the lake's edge. As he approached the water, he felt hopeless and stupid. This was a lake, dammit. The only thing he was going to get if he walked into it was wet.

He cupped a hand and shouted. "Leigh! Leigh! Are you there?"

A very faint cry answered him back, and his heart thumped. He made no sense of the word, but knew the girl's voice. His mind told him that what was happening couldn't be.

A raucus howling broke out behind him, and the hair went up on the back of his neck. Dave pivoted and saw black shadows leaping among the gray ones at the forest's edge. He moved to the water. Something pushed back at him, forcing him away, refusing to let him pass. He sucked in his breath and pivoted around quickly, as gravel crunched, and snarling filled his ears.

Weevils leapt at him. He swung. He cracked the first alongside the head. It crashed yelping into a second, midair, and they both went tumbling. Before they could roll to their paws, Dave bashed one and then the other across the back of the skull.

He stood, trembling, over their bodies. The air scorched over them, and their stench filled his nostrils with a fiery sting. Not dogs or wolves . . . or men, though one had jumped him from a standing position. Werewolves, almost, he thought. Like George had said. Dave took a deep, gulping breath. Mindy's weevils. He hadn't seen one yet in person—and now that he had, he wouldn't forget the crimson glow of their eyes.

He swung back to the curtain across the lake, the one that wouldn't let him pass. Licking dry lips, he moved to the edge. He had to get in, now, before more weevils came.

"I don't believe in this, dammit!" he shouted, and his voice thinned out across the water instead of echoing and carrying. It was as though the fog swallowed up the sound. "But I'm here! I've had damn near everything taken from me . . . Caroline. My youth. Hope. And I'm not too damn brave anymore, either. But I won't let you have her. Leigh belongs here—and I'm coming to get her!"

He shoved his way into the lake. The resistance shattered before him. He gasped as he found himself thigh deep in the cold waters of Spirit Lake. Behind him, the stillness of the forest filled with barks and snaps, and he knew the pack gathered to close in on him. He threw aside the branch and plunged headfirst, swimming toward the fog. Old wives' tales said that evil couldn't cross fresh, running water. Well, old Spirit Lake was dying . . . but it had been a place of power once. It was the only chance he had.

As he swam, his clothes dragged at him, and he cursed his heavy work shoes for making swimming nearly impossible. When his chest heaved and he gasped for breath, he'd nearly reached the fog. It skimmed the lake. Rainbow colors shot through it, giving a pulsating energy.

Dave had almost forgotten about the talisman in his pocket, except that it began to burn, fiercely, hotly, even through the wet cloth of his shirt. It scorched his chest. With a yell of surprise, he treaded water and reached for it.

Hot, yes; burning, yes, but not with flame. It blazed with power and pulsed with a silvery light. It was still folded up within the illustration and neither had been dampened by his swim.

Faced with the impossible, Dave Stoner did a last impossible thing. He threw the talisman into the maw of the fog and shouted, "Leigh! I'm coming after you!" And the man disappeared into the mists.

Caroline bit her lip. Her hands were white knuckled as she gripped the wheel. Over the engine's roar, she heard an angry whine and glanced in the rearview mirror. George twisted around, looking back down the road. His face had paled.

"That's him, all right."

A black-and-red hornet of a car loomed behind them, gaining with every twist of the road. Its tires squealed and sun glinted off its chrome bumpers, blinding her in the mirror. "Another weevil?" She frowned as she guided the ungainly station wagon around another curve and looked for the gravel side road to Spirit Lake.

"Not just another . . . *the* weevil. I think he makes shadows, like copies, of himself. Rosebud says that shadow divided is weaker than the original." George settled uneasily back into the seat, and gripped the barrel of the shotgun tightly. "I think that he's probably the quickest, strongest, and worse of all of them."

And he was stalking me in New York, Caroline thought to herself. She pressed her numb foot harder on the accelerator and the station wagon slid a little on the asphalt road as she swung into another curve. Every bone in her body told her she didn't want to meet *this* one again.

"There!" George grabbed at her elbow. She swung the wheel around and the wagon skewed off the road, spraying gravel and dirt all over.

She'd nearly missed the turnoff. Bushes grew thickly around them and she realized Spirit Lake wasn't as well visited as it had been. There was a high-pitched squealing behind them, cut off abruptly.

"He crashed," said Mindy matter-of-factly.

"No. Not him," George returned. "You sit tight."

The station wagon bucked over the dirt road, springs squeaking and swaying. Caroline fought it, her body sapped by months of illness, her shoulders aching, and wondered why she hadn't let George drive, if he could. Then she knew she couldn't just surrender all of the fight over to the young. It was hers, too. Leigh was still missing.

After long moments, the whining drone of the black-and-red car picked up, hunting them down. A drop of perspiration slid down her forehead, and she was aware Mindy had begun crying softly.

At last the road broke open, and she could see Dave's four-wheel drive parked at the edge. There was no sight of him. The wagon sliced into the dirt next to his and she turned the engine off. In the stillness, the car wheezed and popped and hissed.

George, irritated, said, "Cut it out, Mindy."

"George . . . leave her alone." Caroline put out her arm, found it shaking horribly from weakness, and gathered her littlest daughter in.

George got out of the car. "He's not here," he called back, as he surveyed the area.

Mindy looked up at her mother. Caroline pushed the fringe of bangs to one side and gently patted the tears away.

"I'm sorry, baby," she whispered. "I'm sorry I lied to you about living at the hospital. But I've been too sick and weak to take care of you, and I didn't want you to see me like that. So I thought . . . I thought a summer vacation would be best for you. Do you understand?"

Mindy hugged her fiercely, saying, "I love you, Mommy."

It was answer enough. She forgot about George for a moment until he staggered back to the car door.

"He was here," George gulped. "And the weevils, too."

"Where did he go?"

The boy, nearly a man, shook his head. "I don't know, Mom. What'll we do now?"

Caroline's mouth tightened. "We roll up the windows, lock the doors—and wait."

He fell. His body twisted in surprise, fully expecting to be sucked up into the mist. Instead, the waters opened under him and he fell . . . fell through a sudden black velvet darkness that enveloped him completely, even the involuntary scream from his open mouth, and he was nothing.

He hit with a bone-breaking thump and lay, flat on his back, gasping for breath. His ears popped. Sound flooded in again, though all he could hear was the harsh gasping and the pound of his pulse. He flexed, gingerly, thinking that he was going to have one hell of a bruise, even if nothing was broken.

He sat up. The sky had gone lavender. He sat in a rocky plain. All colors were slate blue and gray, and the rock flowed like a cool lava and reformed even as he watched it. He grew dizzy and looked up to the sky to steady himself.

"Welcome to the nether region, Stoner."

The voice was low and menacing, though smooth and rich. He twisted, and saw a being sitting behind him. The two rock slabs drifted parallel to one another in an ocean of movement.

A weevil, Dave thought. The king of weevils, perhaps, for the being facing him was big and not quite so hairy, a little more manlike. And infinitely more intelligent looking. The glow of his eyes had calmed to a dusky rose, and when he smiled, his fangs flashed whitely.

Dave sat up. He tried to stand, and had to settle for a half-kneeling stance. His battered muscles tensed, ready to jump if the beast jumped for him. "You know who I am. Who are you?"

The beast laughed heartily. He extended a furred hand. "Not so easy, my friend. In this world, names hold power.

You won't be learning my true one. At one time . . . yes, at one time in your world I was called Anubis."

Dave felt his eyes narrow. That had been an Egyptian god. The being toyed with him. "No," he said tightly.

The weevil laughed again. "Appalled? Ashamed that a man would think I was godlike? Where do you think legends come from? Werewolves. Dragons." The beast leaned forward and said even lower, "Unicorns."

"Where are they?" Stoner demanded.

"Oh, they'll be found by you, I have no doubt. You might even get them back through the Gate into your own time and place. There is even a very, very faint possibility you could return the unicorn to her own realm, though I doubt that."

Keep him talking, Stoner thought. He knows a lot and he just might slip and tell me something I can use, something he really doesn't want me to know. "I hope you're not wagering on it. I have all I need to get them through."

"Really? And I was told man was not constitutionally capable of it. I doubted that a little, myself. You see," and the beast leaned close enough that he could smell the smoldering breath, "I have studied your flaws carefully. I find you most . . . interesting. Yes. I was pleased to be able to enter your world once again though my brand of darkness is not normally allowed."

"Flaws?"

The weevil stretched. The sinews grew taut and muscles rippled. Stoner swallowed. He didn't want to have to face that creature down. "What you refer to as flaws are what makes us what we are."

"Yes. The Gate often requires you to sacrifice what you are, if you would pass through it. The little death, it is called."

And what did Leigh sacrifice? And me? Dave shrugged. He looked away from the beast, searching the terrain for the shining aura of a white unicorn, picturing her as George had drawn her for Mindy's book. Out of the corner of his eye, he saw the beast flex to leap, and was on his feet instantly. The beast roared with amusement.

"Well done, Stoner. Well done! Consent to wrestle with me, test my flaws against yours, and I will tell you of the tests the Gate will demand of you and yours. Then, at least, you'll have a fighting chance. You see—I'm as marooned here as you. Breach the Nether Gate, and you'll open up the Twilight Gate for all of us."

"Why not you? Why don't you breach it?"

The weevil looked away. He pulled his lips up in a silent snarl. "I haven't got what it takes," the beast admitted. "The Gate admits the light readily . . . the dark only follows to keep the balance. Yin and yang."

"Tell me where Leigh and the unicorn are."

"In due course. Will you contest with me?"

A stranded weevil was likely to be a hungry one. In this floating ocean of rock and slate, Dave hadn't seen too much either of them could eat . . . except for each other. He wasn't hungry, but from what he'd seen of the carcasses left in back of the Johannsens, the weevils were savage eaters. Was it worth it for the knowledge that would help him pass through the Gate?

Or did the weevil lie to him?

He looked at the hot pink eyes. A tiny drop of saliva dripped from the weevil's fang. Anticipation.

What might Leigh have sacrificed to get this far?

Dave made ready to answer the beast.

EIGHTEEN

"ALL RIGHT."

Before the words had been clearly said, the weevil sprang. Dave braced himself and caught the worst of the blow, tumbling down and out from under his body. The hairy coat of the beast had a greasy feel to it, and he wiped his hands off on his jeans.

The weevil crouched and grinned.

They circled one another. Dave looked into the eyes, then regretted it, for they were flat, like those of a shark, despite their burning quality. The weevil flexed his hands, hairy claws, a travesty of human hands. The nails were hard and curved, black as onyx. The weevil swiped at him, and Dave ducked away from an eyelash-close look at those claws.

As he ducked, he drove in, clipping the beast behind his hock. With a surprised grunt, the weevil went down. As Dave went on top to pin him, the beast flexed and threw him off. He licked his lips.

Dave saw the fear in him and was surprised. Then he thought, *he doesn't expect me to be the aggressor.* With a rush, he followed up his advantage. Again, the weevil threw him off easily enough. The beast had too much sheer bulk for him to master.

An island of rocks slid past. Dave looked over the edge of his island and saw the bubbling molten, ocean they sailed in. It gave him an idea.

He circled the weevil. The beast had regained some of his confidence.

"We are evenly matched, man."

"Perhaps." Dave grinned then. "I seem to have a slight advantage over you."

"Yes? What is it?"

"For some reason, you're afraid of me." Dave lunged then, found himself blocked, then picked up off his feet and thrown. He landed, tumbling, gathered himself, and was up before the weevil could capitalize. Despite the aggressive move, however, the weevil looked desperate. Inside, Dave crowed. He'd hit on something. Perhaps the weevil, a creature of dark and evil, was a born loser. Then he sobered. There was a balance to all things. Dave could as easily be the loser here.

The weevil moved again, his leg sliding out and catching Dave as his hands went to his shoulders, and he struggled to throw him.

Dave shuddered from the grasp that bruised his shoulders, and the scalding breath of the beast. They were locked, face-to-face.

"Since you show such courage," the weevil said, grimacing, "I will give you one of the keys. The little one, born with nothing into this world, must give away her most precious possession."

Little one? Mindy? Dave gritted his teeth as the weevil leaned closer. His muscles seemed to crack with the strain. One push and he'd either be free or so exhausted that the beast would bear him down. Dave heaved.

The weevil's hold broke, and Stoner slid free. He went to one knee again and rolled, groaning as he did so. The rock bit and tore at him, even through his jeans. If the weevil didn't beat him, the rock just might grind him to pieces.

As Dave scrambled to get up, his hand snagged on a piece of paper. A gold-and-silver braided talisman fell out.

Dave scooped it up. The unicorn hair fired his hand, but it was a burning he could withstand this time. He put it in his pocket.

The two stood, each breathing heavily. The weevil shrugged. "I thought I had you, man."

Dave shrugged back. "Don't count your chickens before they hatch."

A heavy, hairy eyebrow went up. "Chickens? Hatch?"

Dave thought. "Maybe a better way of saying it would be, don't count on your meals until they're eaten."

"Ahhh." The weevil snarled in appreciation, his white fangs glistening. "I understand. You humor me. A second key will I give you then. You yourself must use the truth, no matter how it hurts."

Dave felt as though he'd been stabbed. He knew the truth. He knew it more than anyone he'd lived around for years. Was the beast accusing him of living a lie?

His gaze must have flickered, for suddenly, the weevil charged. Dave pivoted, and let the beast's weight bear past him. The weevil's clawed hand went out, and it raked his arm from shoulder to wrist. Blood gushed.

The weevil brought himself up on the rocky edge of the island. He tsked. "So sad, man. Now you will weaken much faster. Our contest is nearly ended."

Dave grabbed his arm. The flesh puckered. Nothing vital was torn, but the slash ran the length of his limb. He was losing blood, and strength, with every minute. He looked past the weevil to the ocean of rock, as another island moved past. It was time for his idea.

"Where I come from," he said with a mental apology to faithful Wolf, "we have pets that look like you. Tufted ears, hairy, usually walk on all fours. They live to be owned by man. They grovel at our feet at night, just to have their ears scratched. They do tricks to please us." A low growling rose, grew louder, threatened to drown his words. The weevil hunched over, his muscles bunching, eyes now a deep, glowing scarlet. "And if a dog so much as growls at us, we kill it."

Snarling, the weevil leapt.

Dave merely moved aside. The beast lunged past him, through the air, and off the end of the island. With a scream, he clawed to halt his plunge into the molten rock. He caught the promontory and hung, desperately, his claws scrabbling.

Dave walked to the end of the island and leaned over, looking down. He fished the talisman out and showed it. "This burns me, but I'm willing to bet that it will hurt you a lot worse. Am I right?" He waved it in the weevil's face, and the beast flinched. Dave held it over the paw that anchored him to the boulder. "Now you tell me, very quickly, where Leigh and the unicorn are."

"I don't know."

But the weevil's gaze gave him away. Dave saw him glance to a not-too-far range, where the land seemed stable. He could get there, if he was willing to do some rock hopping.

"And the rest."

The weevil licked his lips. "George drew us here. He must set us free. Leigh must let go of her fondest dream. The unicorn must take instead of give . . . and Caroline—"

"Yes—"

"The woman must give up living for dying."

Dave sucked in his breath. Then, angrily, he plunged the talisman onto the weevil's paw. With a hiss of seared flesh and a yelp of pain, the beast let go. He dropped onto a very small boulder and was carried away, howling, "Just remember . . . the Gate will open for me as well."

Dave yelled after the creature. "I'd hold on very tight, if I were you."

His hands were shaking as he replaced the talisman in

his pocket. A hot wetness blurred his vision and he muttered as he tore his other sleeve off and tried to afix a kind of bandage around his arm, "Lies. All lies. Especially about Carrie."

When he was done, he sat down quickly, as his legs literally gave out from under him. He needed to rest, he thought, looking at the far-away mountain. Then he would find Leigh and the unicorn. He closed his eyes.

His lids snapped back open. Shock. He was suffering from shock, of a kind, and it would slow him down if he stayed here. He had to keep moving. That, he knew about. With a sigh, Dave began pacing the island, looking for the next jump close enough to make.

Legs trembling, hands scrapped raw, and his right arm now nearly useless, he made the last jump, and hugged the shore of the blue-gray mountain. He looked up, seeing the caves and valleys. More weevils? Other dangers? Wearily, he put his cheek to the glassy surface. Maybe. He couldn't care about those.

Cupping his hands, he cried out, "Leigh! Leigh! Are you here?"

Two figures moved out from the rock, stalking a frosty white beast of mythology and light. The unicorn looked to him with frantic violet eyes. "Choose! We must choose the right Leigh or we'll never get back."

Dave staggered to a halt as the two girls paused in their harrowing of the unicorn and turned to look at him. Neither of them was Leigh. His heart hammered in his throat. His eyes blurred. "Dear God, not again."

The two Asian girls moved forward, rice bowls in their hands, fathomless brown eyes unrevealing of their souls. One of them, he knew, would have a live grenade buried underneath the rice in her offering. Now he remembered what he had only remembered in his dreams. Now he knew what he had buried and dared not face, even though he had lost Caroline and his youth because of it. Now he knew what it was that tore him from his sleep with agonizing gasps every night. One of the girls was the one he had killed in Vietnam, to save his unit, tearing away his sanity in the doing.

"Choose!"

"I can't, goddammit! Not again." Dave hung on to the last scrap of his mind. He rubbed his hand over his face. He would not kill again. Suddenly he lunged for both of the rice bowls, and hugged them to his chest, knocking the girls aside. "This time, I'm the one who dies!" he cried.

The weevils swarmed around the station wagon. Mindy's fright had cried itself dry an hour ago, and she sat, small and pale, her Bambi eyes swollen in her face. George gripped the shotgun tighter.

"If I roll down the window just enough to poke the barrel out—"

"They'd tear the gun out of your hands and then come for us. No. We're going to sit right here." Caroline squeezed a little closer to Mindy, who sniffled.

"I'm thirsty, Mommy. It's hot in here."

"I know, honey."

The beasts stood up now and then to look in. And they circled, endlessly. Through the air vents, their stench and heat seeped in, and George thought he was going to vomit. The red-and-black car had vanished into the smoke of evil from which it had been made, and the weevil issuing from it had multiplied itself into a pack. For an hour or so, they'd been at this stalemate.

All at once, all six of the beasts stood up. Three on one side. Three on the other.

"Uh-oh," George said. He straightened.

The weevils put out their pawlike hands, placed them on the windows, and began to push. Back and forth. Back and forth. The station wagon rocked under the assault. Side to side, more and more.

"They're going to flip us!" George cried.

The wagon shuddered violently and began to go, on Caroline's side. With a scream, the three of them fell as the vehicle went over. They twisted and turned and tumbled. Mindy shrieked in terror, then collided with the dashboard and went horribly limp.

George's doorframe, warped, popped open. George got to his knees and blasted the first beast that reached for them. It splattered and bile rose in his throat at the sight and stench of the shattered flesh. His shoulder felt black and blue and as another snarling face poked in, he closed his eyes and let rip with the second barrel. At his back, he heard his mother crying softly, "Mindy, Mindy."

He forced his eyes open and, trembling, pulled the dead shells out and tried to put two new ones in. A snarling beast reached in and grabbed the gun's barrel, and pulled it from his hands.

George swore and scrambled after it, determined not to lose the shotgun. As he reached after it, into the open air, a weevil latched onto his arms. With a steady, gutteral sound, and inhuman strength, the beast hauled him from the overturned car.

"Mom!" he screamed as he was borne slowly into the late afternoon, awaited by slavering, red-eyed weevils.

Caroline saw her son being dragged from the car and let go of Mindy's limp form. She threw herself after him and grabbed him by the ankles, even as she knew she would fail. Her frail strength had been sapped just driving here. The cancer, and the cure, had left her nothing to fight with. George's body tightened and she felt herself being dragged from the car, too.

Her son had stopped screaming. Her own breath caught in her throat, wondering if they had slit his throat already.

The beasts grew strangely quiet.

George said, "Let go, Mom. Get back in the car. It's me they want."

She swallowed tightly. She had only her toes gripping her to the doorframe of the vehicle. "I can't, honey. You're my son. If it's you they want . . ." She let go and stood up slowly, George dropping to the ground, "It's me they've got to go through."

"Mom!" George rolled over, white-hot tears cascading over his face. "Don't do this to me! This is all my fault. They came out of me, out of—out of what I did. I drew all the weevils, I gave them their Gate, out of my mind. I had to or, or . . . or explode. Mom, I was responsible for the crash!" The words tumbled out of him, tearing out of his throat before it closed tight, locking the rest of his words away.

"George," she said softly, her eyes locked with the gazes of the weevils. "Listen to me. You weren't responsible for your father's death. He did what he wanted to, his whole life. He was the father and you were the son. You didn't fail him. George, I saw the reports. You were buckled in on the passenger side. You just don't remember everything that happened. He drove through the night, even though he shouldn't have."

"Mom," George said miserably. "Don't lie."

She did not turn her face to him. "George, we may be about to die. I wouldn't lie to you now. You did nothing wrong. Now get the shotgun," she added as she moved forward.

She held out her hands. She slipped a little in the gore of the two weevils George had shot. Even as she watched, one of the weevils wavered and divided, renewing their number. "Get inside and take care of Mindy," she ordered.

Crying freely, he crawled back inside the car. He dug for the book, hands shaking, but he had nothing to draw with. And no idea of what to do. Was he free? Had he been purged with the truth? Did he dare trust his mother's words? Tears obliterated the pages in front of him. Darkness filled his vision. George froze, book in hand. It was not lies that filled the book. It was something bigger, something worse, something he could not understand even as it tried to storm out of it. He dared not sketch anything. He had no control over his visions. He would destroy them all.

Outside, with a shudder, Caroline waited for the weevils to do whatever it was they planned to do.

Thunder cracked. It exploded around them, and Caroline screamed sharply with pain, looking over the lake. The rainbow mist boiled violently, and the weevils scattered.

A white unicorn galloped out of the cloud, bearing a man and a girl on her back. She raced across the air as though it were solid, her mane ruffling in a celestial breeze, her hooves sending sparks of lightning. As she plunged to the earth, the weevils fell back, growling and slavering. She whinnied and threatened them with her horn of gold and ivory as she beat a path to the battered car.

Caroline sobbed with joy at the sight of her daughter. "Leigh!"

George scrambled out of the car. He leaned back in and dragged out a drowsy Mindy in his arms. She clutched tightly to her book. She pointed triumphantly. "I told you she had a horn!"

The rainbow pulsed around them. Dave slid off the unicorn, held his arms up, and caught Leigh off the unicorn's back. There was a moment's pause as if the girl did not wish to dismount, then Leigh slipped into his arms and ran to her mother. They held each other tightly.

Caroline looked at Dave over her daughter's head. Her daughter was almost as tall, and she found it difficult to do. Words stuck in her throat. The man looked at her solemnly, then nodded. "I know," he said.

The unicorn danced before them. She snorted mightily in triumph, keeping the weevils cowed and scattered. "You have passed great trials," she said. "And I have regained much of my power. The Gate has been forced open, but only a crack. Send me back—I beg of you. Right the wrong that you have done, and send me back."

Leigh stammered, "But I—"

"No, child. Not just you."

George fisted the tears from his face. "I don't know what to do."

The unicorn bowed her head. "Then we are all doomed."

"Keys," Dave said suddenly. His deep voice cracked a little, and he swallowed. "I have keys to the Gate. I wrestled the weevil for them." He cradled his bandaged right arm in his left. "George must give away his secrets."

Rosebud turned to George. She looked at him deeply with her long-lashed violet eyes.

"I—I don't know. I don't have any secrets!"

About them, the ring of furred and musky evil growled louder. Fangs gnashed. The shadows multiplied until George knew that even Rosebud could not stay them. He looked at Mindy. He thought of what it was he might have drawn at their last moment. "I thought . . . I thought I had been driving the car. I thought it was my fault he died. He made fun of me all the time, Mom. How much my voice had started cracking. He was always telling me I couldn't do anything right. He wanted to throw away my sketches. He wanted me to be a jock. He'd lie to me. How he'd promise to let me drive and then take it back when I went out with him. He told me I'd never be good enough for him. He told me about the girlfriends he had on his sales trips and laughed at you. He said I'd never be as much man as him." George took a deep, gulping breath. "I thought he'd come back to haunt me, to haunt us. And I hated him for it! Because I was glad he was gone. Oh, God, Mom, he was my dad and I loved him sometimes, but mostly I hated him, and that's the truth." Tears glistened. He thought of Sun Ling and what he had said about art. "That's what shows in the pictures, isn't it? All that hatred. It came from me! I did all this."

"Hatred is a strong emotion, but it's not evil." His mother reached for him.

George backed away, shamefaced, and Caroline had to stretch to put her arm around him. "It's my fault, too. I knew he wasn't a good father. I knew he took out his frustrations on you. I kept hoping . . . I kept hoping things would get better." She added shakily, "The truth sets you free. And once you're past that . . . you'll be able to remember the good times you had with your dad. There were good ones, too. Just . . . give yourself a chance."

The unicorn kissed him and smacked her lips at the salt on his face. George put a shaky hand to her muzzle.

"Nobody evil could ever have put me to paper," the beast said. "The love came out as well as the hatred." She nudged him. "Remember that."

The weevils stood at bay, drooling and snarling. The unicorn danced a little, showing them her hooves. "Quickly," she warned.

Dave felt dead on his feet, as indeed he should have been, but the explosion from the bomb in the rice bowl that he'd taken had blasted open the Gate instead of his body. He felt as if the fire had burned part of him away. He ached everywhere. He looked at her and repeated with effort what the evil creature had told him. "And Leigh must give away her dreams."

Leigh, pale and disturbed, her hair a gentle gold falling to her shoulders, shook her head in bewilderment.

"There must be something," Rosebud prompted.

"I wanted a horse more than anything in the world. I wanted the freedom and the beauty. Let me go with you."

The two stared into one another's faces, unicorn to innocent girl, and as the silence stretched, Leigh's face lost hope of an answer. "Nothing," she said, "will ever be as wonderful as you."

"You can't know that," the mare said.

"I can't know that it will! We had magic, and you're taking it away with you."

"There is magic here, Leigh." Rosebud nudged her. "The challenge is keeping a heart open enough to be able to search for it. A sacrifice is not a sacrifice unless there is some pain and nobility in it."

"Then tell me what I can give up to keep you."

The unicorn lowered her head further, the ivory and gold-shot horn coming so close as to slice Leigh's forehead, but stopping short. Caroline held her breath. Dave took her hand and found it icy.

Leigh did not flinch. "I'm not good enough."

"No, child. You're too good, and this world has a great need of such goodness. You're wanted here."

"What about what I want! I want wonder and mystery. I want to know that I am something beyond the touch of mere earth. . . ."

"All I can leave you is memory. Isn't it better to have memory than to have nothing?"

Leigh let out her breath with a shaky noise. Her expression crumpled in defeat. "I'm not sure," she said. "But I guess I'll have to find out."

George saw the aurora waver. He forgot himself and Leigh's dilemma as the sky itself made a moaning noise. Something dark and gigantic grew in its wake. "Damn," he said. "It's coming!"

Dave swallowed tightly. "Mindy must give up her greatest possession."

Rosebud looked to the little girl. She seemed to smile in a horsy way. "That we will save for last. Now for Caroline."

"No." Dave moved, suddenly, to move between them. "She's already given up everything."

The unicorn reared, striking the hot summer air, which had suddenly chilled. "The deeds must be done! Already I feel the Gate yielding! Quickly! Before it is too late, for one comes from the Gate after me, and this one you defeated once in battle, man, but you will not defeat again!"

The weevil called Anubis. Dave felt his face burn, and he would not, could not, look at Carrie. In desperation, he said, "Caroline must give up living for dying."

She went cold hearing those words. Then she took a deep breath. "Then I must let go of you, unicorn . . . eternity for mortality. I have to accept that the doctors are doing all they can. No magical touches. Welcome to the real world." She coughed harshly.

Rosebud nodded. "Touch me," the beast whispered in her rich contralto voice. "For it is you who must heal me."

Trembling, Caroline reached out and stroked the silvery coat of the beautiful creature. Rosebid lipped gently at her bare wrist. "I'm sorry," Caroline whispered. "They did it out of love. That's the secret. Go back where you belong."

Then the unicorn turned to Dave. "You now."

"But I don't understand what it means for me."

"Say it."

"I'm to use the truth, no matter how it hurts."

"Then do it."

He swallowed. The children watched him. Tall George, on the brink of manhood, his face streaked with dried tears. Pale Leigh, a younger, more beautiful version of her mother. And then there was Mindy, fine hair of sable, with bangs fringing eyes that mirrored . . . mirrored . . . his thoughts plunged to a halt. He knew that stubborn jut of chin so well. He faced it nearly every morning when he shaved. Staggered, he looked to Caroline, his face stark.

Caroline said softly, "The truth stands in front of you, Dave. Say it. You must. For all of us."

Stricken, he looked back and forth. "I can't do it. I won't hurt the children."

Mindy stamped her foot. "You don't care about us! You don't! I know you don't! Because you loved Mommy, and you still love her, and if you were still married to her, we wouldn't even exist!" Her voice went shrill. She clutched her book as if her heart was breaking.

"No," he said quietly, and reached out his hand to her. "No, Mindy. That's not true. I love all of you very much." He bent down, dark brown head to brunette head. "And this is true, too . . . Mindy . . . I'm your father."

Leigh let out a tiny gasp. She looked from her sister to Stoner, and then staggered back into George as she realized what she heard was true.

Mindy tilted her head. "Daddy was my daddy."

"No, baby," Caroline said, her throat tight with pain. "Before . . . before you were a seed in me, Daddy left me. He was going to get a divorce, he said. I sent George and Leigh away to camp for the summer. I . . . I was all alone, and then Dave accidentally met me in New York. We . . . we realized we still loved each other. But then, Daddy came back. We didn't want to hurt anybody, so Dave left again. It wasn't until later that I realized . . . I realized I was carrying a baby. You. Dave's baby."

"And you never told me," Stoner said lowly.

Caroline couldn't stand to look at him. "No. I couldn't. I know what it would have meant to you. And . . . Chris was always talking about leaving me again. Then, after the accident, it was just too complicated to undo. Oh, God." She looked at all of them, and began to cry. "Please forgive me. I sent them to you this summer hoping that you'd love them and they'd love you and that somehow—somehow, I could make it all right."

Thunder rolled ominously. Rosebud threw up her head in alarm. "Time has run out. The last gift. Mindy . . . your book."

The little girl stood frozen to the ground. Then she said, "No."

"The book is the final phase of the Gate. It summoned me here. It must send me back."

"No! George gave it to me."

George got to his knees and tried to take the girl in his arms, but Mindy shrugged him away. Helpless, he said, "I'll make you another one, honey."

"No. My mommy is dying. If my daddy isn't my daddy, then you're probably not my brother! No! It's my book and I won't give it away! I hate you. I hate all of you!" Mindy shoved George violently aside. She turned to duck back inside the overturned car.

Dave caught her. He paled at the impact on his wounded arm. The tall man and the little girl eyed one another.

He said, "When I left to get Leigh . . . you ran outside, remember? And you gave me a hug and said you loved me."

Mindy's gaze dropped. She nodded, her chin trembling.

"And I love you, too. I would never do anything to hurt you."

"Prove it."

"Tell me how."

Mindy took a long, shaky breath. "Love Mommy, too. Love Mommy like you were always supposed to."

Stoner looked at Caroline. Her scarf turban had fallen, lost somewhere in the depths of the car. Her beautiful pale gold hair had dulled. It was half gone, the pink skin of baldness from the chemotherapy shining through. She'd lost the girlish blush to her cheeks. There were sharp lines in her face. Fatigue and pain had left purplish bruises under her eyes. And Dave Stoner thought he'd never seen anyone quite so beautiful.

"I do love her. I loved her enough to let her go twice. This time, too, if I have to. I'll let you all go."

"No!" said George, getting up from the ground. "Mindy . . . the secret isn't just my drawing. It's the paper. Remember what Sun Ling said. It's prayer paper. What we want most in our souls. Something to scare us because we thought we were evil—and something to save us because we needed help! We have to send it away. It's meant to go." He wrenched the book from her and searched the ground. He plucked up a seared, burned-off twig and began sketching. Hope fueled him this time instead of hatred. The charcoal drawing was crude, but recognizable. All of them, holding hands, facing a unicorn as it leapt into a rainbow. "The best we can wish is to send Rosebud home. And we'll be all right. I promise."

Mindy launched herself onto her brother's chest, burrowing fiercely. "Do you promise, George?"

"We all promise."

She bit her lip, twisted about, and then threw her book into the air, crying, "Rosebud! I love you, too!"

Amidst the roll of thunder and strike of lightning, the unicorn leapt to impale the book on her horn. With a trumpeting neigh of triumph, she pivoted.

The lake had turned leaden, gray and dull. It boiled up at her as if gaining a body to strike. Above it, the aurora borealis curtain began to part. Red smoldering eyes sprang out at her.

An immense wolflike face snarled. The unicorn struck, once, with her horn, and it whispered away into smoke. The Gateway stood clear.

They heard her shout of joy. "Home!"

And then the Twilight Gate slammed shut.

With a whoosh of black smoke, the earth-born weevils were sucked up into the fog. It sank into itself and disappeared.

Stoner reached out his left arm and took his love into his embrace. The three children watched silently for a moment, then joined in the embrace, an echo of George's last drawing. All went quiet on the shore of Spirit Lake.

From far away, thunder boomed again, and the rain began to fall. The lake mirrored its striking. Caroline pointed. The waters began to clear. She threw back her head and took a deep breath into her scarred lungs.

Between light and dark, lies twilight.
Between despair and healing, must lie hope.

"Oh, God," she said. "At last I can believe in miracles!"

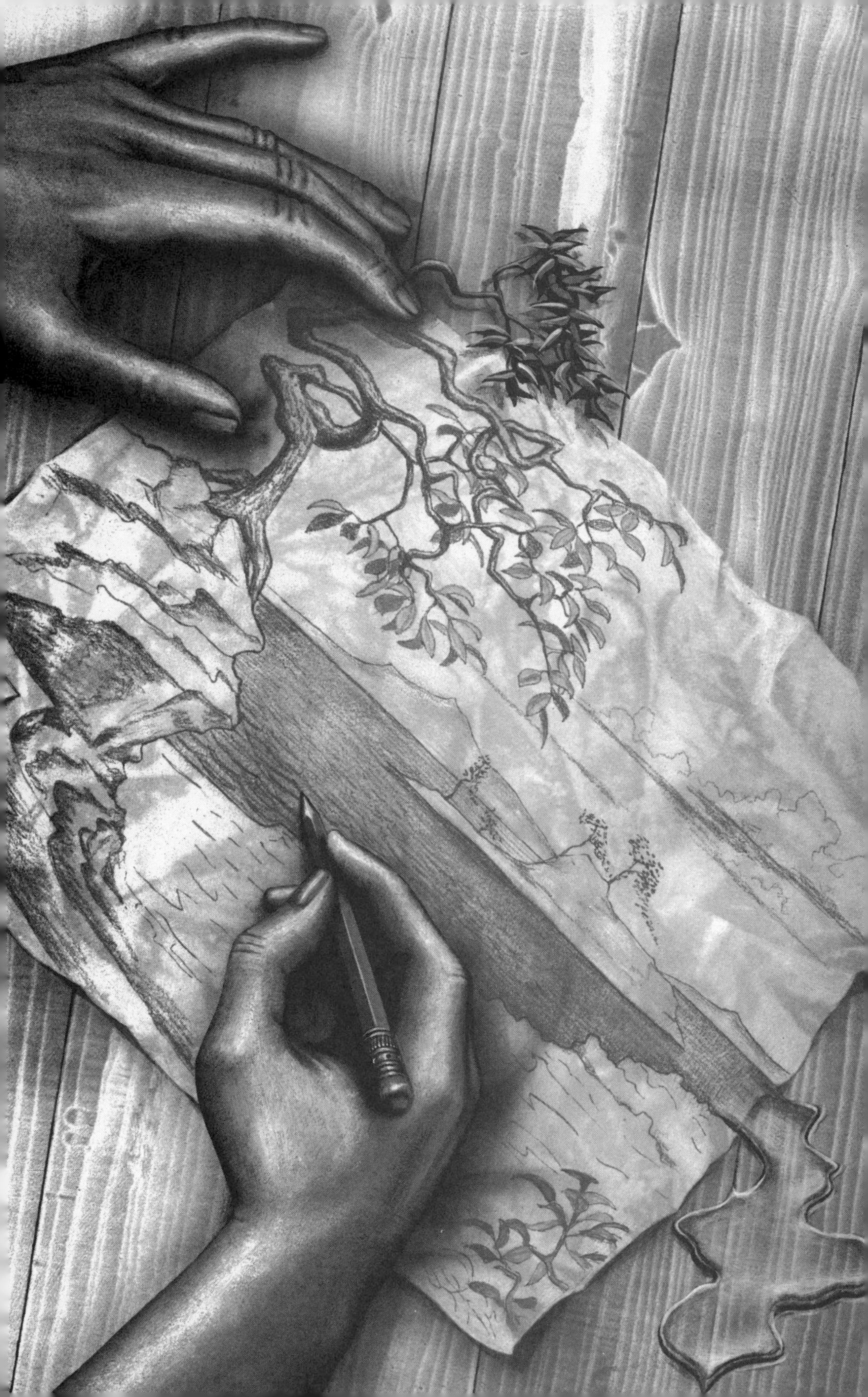

NINETEEN

CAROLINE CRADLED GEORGE UNder one arm and Mindy with the other as the four-wheel drive bumped along the back road, heading out of a pink-lemonade dawn. Leigh sat in the front, a faraway look on her face as the landscape passed by. She felt dim and almost nonexistent. Everyone else had gotten something: Mindy a real father, George forgiveness, her mother hope, Stoner a family. She was the only one who'd really given anything away. It was not fair. There would never be anything like the unicorn in her life again.

George moved forward slightly. He whispered so that only Leigh could hear him, "If there are unicorns, Leigh, somewhere there must be dragons and gryphons and gorgons, too. And sphinxes who know the answer to everything."

She turned to look at him and tried to smile. "Pshaw, right," she said back. Her brother smiled.

George felt his mother stroke his temple.

"Secrets are heavy if they're carried alone."

His throat felt as though he'd used it for a Cuisinart. "How could I tell you? How could I?"

"Because you love and trust me."

His mouth twisted. "You didn't want Dad to

give me driving lessons so early, remember? You used to fight about it."

"In those days," Caroline said faintly, "we fought about everything. Anyway, I thought you were too young."

"I was fourteen and a half! Almost old enough for a permit. And Dad didn't want to be embarrassed when he took me in to get tested for one. Said I should know what the world was about."

"And do you?"

He shook his head wearily. "No. And it wasn't the accident, anyway, was it? It was the bad feelings we left behind."

"Let them go."

"I'm trying. I'm still learning."

"Good. Try to keep it that way for, oh, say, the next thirty or forty years."

He could feel her shift position and knew she had looked up at Stoner. "Yeah," he answered. "I guess you're never too old to learn a thing or two."

Stoner murmured, "So it was the paper. I got that paper in Thailand. We saved a village just over the border when we were lost. I never thought anything of it. I gave it to you for your sketches."

"And I never used it," Caroline said. "I let George use it after the accident. The drawing seemed to be good therapy for him. . . . "

"Yeah," George said again. "Be careful what you wish for . . . you just might get it."

Mindy said sleepily, "I have a page left. I tore it out, just in case." She pulled a folded-up wad from her jeans pocket.

George sat up. He looked at the paper.

Dave reached over and touched it. "The lake," he said.

"And those jerks trying to buy it from you," George said nastily, and grinned broadly. "Just one more time."

Leigh groaned. "Oh, no."

"Yes. But don't worry. This time we know what we're doing. And don't forget. The secret is love. Right, Mom?"

Caroline sighed. "I certainly hope so."

Between light and dark, lies twilight,
Between despair and healing, must lie hope.